P9-DHP-777

"This is the most amazing gift I've ever received."

Melanie swallowed an unexpected knot of emotion. "No one has ever done anything like this," she said, looking at the pine dresser Adam had made for her.

She lowered her head, blinking at the moisture welling in her eyes.

Adam laid a rough fingertip along her cheek and gently urged her to look up at him.

"I'm glad you like it," he said, his voice lowered, a soft smile curving his lips.

"It's beautiful." She gave in to an impulse and threw her arms around his neck.

It was supposed to be a quick hug.

But as she drew away, her hands rested on his shoulders. He held her by the arms, and their eyes met in a connection that was almost physical in intensity.

She wanted to move away.

She wanted to be drawn into his arms.

Melanie hesitated, lost in the confused back-and-forth of longing and reality.

Books by Carolyne Aarsen

Love Inspired

CAROLYNE AARSEN

lives in Alberta on a small ranch with her husband and the youngest of their four children. Carolyne's writing skills have been honed between being a stay-at-home mom, wife, foster mother, columnist and business partner with her husband in their logging operation and cattle ranch. Writing for Love Inspired has given her the wonderful opportunity to combine her love of the Lord with her love of a romantic story.

TOWARD HOME

CAROLYNE AARSEN

Published by Steeple Hill Books™

If you purchased this book without a cover you should be aware that this book is stolen property. It was reported as "unsold and destroyed" to the publisher, and neither the author nor the publisher has received any payment for this "stripped book."

STEEPLE HILL BOOKS

Steeple
Hill™

ISBN 0-373-87222-4

TOWARD HOME

Copyright © 2003 by Carolyne Aarsen

All rights reserved. Except for use in any review, the reproduction or utilization of this work in whole or in part in any form by any electronic, mechanical or other means, now known or hereafter invented, including xerography, photocopying and recording, or in any information storage or retrieval system, is forbidden without the written permission of the editorial office, Steeple Hill Books, 233 Broadway, New York, NY 10279 U.S.A.

All characters in this book have no existence outside the imagination of the author and have no relation whatsoever to anyone bearing the same name or names. They are not even distantly inspired by any individual known or unknown to the author, and all incidents are pure invention.

This edition published by arrangement with Steeple Hill Books.

® and TM are trademarks of Steeple Hill Books, used under license. Trademarks indicated with ® are registered in the United States Patent and Trademark Office, the Canadian Trade Marks Office and in other countries.

Visit us at www.steeplehill.com

Printed in U.S.A.

Come to me, all you who are weary and burdened, and I will give you rest.

—*Matthew* 11:28

To Ann Leslie Tuttle,
who helped me shape this book,
and to Karen Solem, who gave me
timely and valuable advice.

Chapter One

"I sure hope *this* is the place." Melanie glanced once more at the wrinkled map her supervisor had given her, then at the unmarked mailbox teetering at the end of the driveway.

Supposedly Helen Engler, her next patient, lived here. It had taken her half an hour with two wrong turns and directions from a young woman out riding her horse to find the place.

She turned into the driveway bordered by willows on one side, swooping poplars on the other. Puzzlement was overridden by happy memories of this place as she finally recognized the driveway. When she used to visit here she had come from a different direction.

It had been fourteen years since she'd lived in the town of Derwin, yet she knew she had been here before. She was also sure that she knew the name Engler. But the name and the place didn't mesh in her memory.

She rounded the last bend into an opening and came to a stop in front of a Victorian-style house.

A deep porch shaded the front and side of the house, its curved pillars creating a sturdy, welcoming place. Gingerbread trimmed the large bay window across the front, echoing the trim above the dormer windows perched along the top floor. Brightly colored petunias and lobelia spilled from baskets hung from the ceiling of the porch, giving it a festive, welcoming air.

But best of all, set alongside the house, flowing out from it and softening the angles, stood a turret topped with a conical roof. The four-sided tower overlooked the yard sheltered with deep green spruce and aspen.

Melanie stepped out of the car, a thrill of pleasure and surprise coursing through her.

It *was* the house of those childhood dreams, Melanie thought with a smile, hitching the strap of her briefcase over her shoulder. The Shewchuks must have sold the house, and now it belonged to the Englers.

Melanie took a moment to listen to the sighing of the wind in the trees surrounding the house, her mind sifting back fourteen years. Her good friend Dena Shewchuk had lived here and Melanie had been envious not only of her large family, but of Dena's house. A home.

The same home her wandering father had always promised Melanie and her mother.

As a child Melanie had woven countless daydreams around this home. She had promised herself that someday she would have a house, a home exactly like the Shewchuks. The memory had stayed with her during the intervening years.

But as she walked closer to the house, reality intruded on her memories. Blistered paint peeled off the house's wooden siding, dust coated the windows. The weeds choking the flower bed were an ironic contrast to the flowerpots decorating the porch.

She had taken a few steps up the porch stairs when she heard the deep sound of a man's voice. Curious, she walked along the veranda to the yard beside the house.

Sunlight, diffused through the softly swaying aspen trees overhead, dappled the two figures on a lawn that had been hidden from view. A tiny girl about three years of age threw a bright blue ball to a man who sat only a few feet away from her. The little girl wore pale pink coveralls, the man blue jeans and a white T-shirt.

As Melanie watched the idyllic scene, the little girl suddenly turned away, trundling toward the back of the house, her curls bouncing on her shoulders.

''Tiffany,'' the man called out. ''Come back here, sweetie.'' But the little girl, now gone, didn't come back, nor did she respond.

The man pushed himself to his feet to follow her. From where she stood Melanie caught his expression of pain, at odds with the charming scene she had just witnessed.

He stopped as soon as he saw Melanie, lifting his hand to shade his eyes.

"Hello," Melanie called out. "I'm Melanie Visser. The health nurse. I've come to see Helen Engler."

The man walked up the three steps on the side of the veranda and as he came toward her, Melanie took a small step back.

"I'm Adam Engler. Helen's son." His handshake was firm, solid, his height on the borderline of intimidating.

The introduction wasn't necessary. Adam Engler had, one time, been as much a part of her dreams as this house and the Shewchuk family.

His once-blond hair had deepened to a sandy color, but he still wore it a little long, curling at the ends. His deep blue eyes that had once sparkled with fun and enthusiasm now looked older. Sadder.

However, they held hers with a faint intensity, his head angled to one side, as if studying her.

He didn't remember her, she realized with a brush of regret. And why should he? When he'd come to her rescue those many years ago, she had been a mere junior high student. He an exalted high school sophomore.

"My mother is in the house," Adam continued. "Just come around the back with me. I have to make sure Tiffany went inside."

Adam half turned, gesturing for Melanie to go ahead of him. As she passed him she chanced another glance, trying to reconcile this older, harder man with the laughing teenager of her memories. To her increasing confusion, Adam looked directly down at her, a faint frown tugging at his sandy-colored eyebrows as if he was searching for the memory Melanie had found.

As they approached the back door, Adam reached past her to pull it open, his arm brushing hers.

Melanie resisted the urge to pull back, flashing him what she hoped was a casually thankful smile before she entered the porch. She blamed her bemusement on an assault of memories. This house and unexpectedly meeting Adam, a young man from a happier time in her life.

She stepped past a small pair of sandals the same size as the running shoes lying haphazardly beside them. They looked lost on the large porch that Melanie remembered chockablock with shoes, boots and the occasional pair of wet socks.

As she stepped into the spacious kitchen, her hungry eyes flitted over the room, revisiting other memories.

The walls were more scarred, the floor more scuffed. The counters that followed the two walls no longer sparkled, the white paint dulled by collected grime.

In spite of the neglect, the room still exuded the same welcoming atmosphere. The bay window with its deep seat still invited a lonely soul to sit in it and look out over the secluded yard.

A feeling of melancholy filled her. Mixed through that was an emotion she experienced only when she thought of Derwin.

Homesickness.

A tiny woman sat at a large wooden table beside the bay window, a walker standing beside her chair.

Bright blue eyes looked up at Melanie, magnified by a pair of wire-rimmed glasses. Soft brown hair threaded with gray curled around her smiling face. Beside her chair stood the little girl Melanie had seen with Adam.

"I'm Melanie Visser. I'm sorry I'm late," Melanie said, walking over to Helen Engler. "I got turned around on the way here."

"It is a bit hard to find," Helen agreed, reaching up to shake Melanie's hand. Her handshake was as firm and brisk as her son's. "I'm obviously Helen. And this little angel is my granddaughter, Tiffany." Helen brushed the little girl's blond hair back and clipped a barrette into her curls. "I take it you and Adam have already met." She leaned back in her chair, and her smile twisted into a grimace of pain.

"How long have you been up?" Melanie asked, pulling up a chair beside Helen.

"Only a few minutes. I knew what time you were coming and I wanted to be ready for you. The doctor told me I could sit up for a little while."

Melanie laid the back of her hand against Helen's cheek. She felt a bit warm, but nothing to be alarmed about.

"I told her to stay in bed," Adam said.

"That's okay. She needs to get up once in a while." Melanie opened her bag and drew out Helen's file and the blood pressure cuff.

"But she just came out of the hospital yesterday. Should she even be sitting up?"

Melanie heard the faint note of anxiety in Adam's voice and took it for what it was. A concerned son.

"Actually she should," Melanie murmured. "If Helen doesn't move around enough, she runs the risk of developing blood clots, which is far more serious than being a little overtired." She turned back to Helen. "I'm going to take your blood pressure now. Do you mind pushing your sleeve up?"

Helen's blood pressure seemed a little high.

"Have you been taking your medication?" Melanie rolled up the cuff and made a note in her file.

Helen nodded.

"I think we'll need to make a change. I'll contact the doctor for a new prescription."

"The doctor told me this might happen," Helen offered, as she buttoned up her cuff. "He said not to make any sudden changes."

"He's right. Now I'm going to ask you a few more questions, if you don't mind."

Helen answered them in a steady quiet voice, glancing over at her son once in a while.

Adam pulled up a chair and rested his elbows on the table. Melanie didn't look his way as she wrote down Helen's answers, but she felt completely aware of him.

"Gramma sick?" Tiffany clutched the armrest of Helen's chair, her head tilted up to Melanie.

"Gramma had surgery, sweetie," Adam said from his end of the table.

Tiffany frowned, still looking at Melanie.

Melanie leaned a little closer, smiling at the little girl. "The technical term for that is 'owwie,'" she said with a wink.

"Gramma has an owwie." Tiffany nodded, as if understanding this.

"I see I'm going to have to brush up on my medical terminology," Adam said dryly as he got up.

Melanie slanted Adam a puzzled glance, surprised to see the faint hint of a dimple hovering at the corner of his mouth.

"Can I get you a cup of coffee?" he asked.

"No. Thank you."

"But I bet you want a cookie, don't you, Tiff?" Adam scooped up his daughter as Melanie concentrated on what she was doing. As Melanie and Helen chatted, she tried to ignore Adam rummaging through the cupboard, pulling out a cookie for his daughter.

It was the potent combination of Adam and this house, Melanie thought, blaming her edgy mood on this place. It had occupied so much of her dreams. To see it so run-down, so neglected bothered her.

She turned her attention back to Helen.

"Just to fill me in, how did you break your hip?"

Helen glanced over at Adam, her teeth worrying her lip. "I fell, uh, while…changing a lightbulb."

Adam spun around, dropping the bag of cookies on the counter. "I thought you told me you slipped in the bathtub?"

Helen waved her hand, as if brushing away his anger. "I guess you didn't hear me right."

"I guess you were lying to me."

The tension was rising and Melanie intervened. "Speaking of the bathroom, I need to see what you need in terms of bathing assistance." Melanie closed the file and tucked it into her bag. She didn't know why Helen had lied to Adam about how she'd injured herself and it wasn't really her problem. "Here are some exercises that the physiotherapist drew up for you," Melanie said. "I'd like to go over them with you in a few minutes. You can do the first ones in your bed."

Adam looked over his mother's shoulder, his eyes still narrowed with anger. "Exercises so soon? It's only been a bit more than a week since her surgery."

"It's all about keeping the muscles toned and healthy and her new hip working. We want your mother to recuperate as fast as possible."

"I'm with you there," Adam said. "I don't need her hurting herself in this house again."

"I'm hoping to be able to get back to my garden. And maybe you can get some work done on the house, Adam," Helen said.

"We won't be here that long." Adam's voice held a note of warning as he straightened, his hands on his hips. "The sooner I get you out of this place, the better."

"It was one little fall. And if you'd been here I wouldn't have had to change the lightbulb. Remember the doctor said no sudden changes." Helen turned back to Melanie. "Adam wants me to move to Calgary. As soon as possible."

Melanie frowned. "What do you mean, as soon as possible?"

"Next week." Helen sat back, her arms crossed over her chest. "And I shouldn't go, should I?"

"It's too early to be thinking of that, that's for sure," Melanie said.

"I told you, Adam." Helen threw him a triumphant glance, which Adam ignored. "This is such a beautiful spot. Don't you agree, Melanie?"

"It's a lovely house," Melanie agreed carefully, sensing from the frown on Adam's face and the pleading look in Helen's that she was venturing into a point of dispute between mother and son. "I always admired it as a little girl."

Helen's face brightened. "Have you been here before?"

"When I was young I used to visit the Shewchuk family here." Melanie couldn't help but smile at the memory and the coincidence of sitting here in the same kitchen she had spent so many happy hours in.

"You lived in Derwin?" Adam asked.

Melanie looked up at him, her mind calling back that silly schoolgirl crush with surprising ease. "Yes, I did. For about fourteen months. That was a while ago."

"And you knew the Shewchuks."

"I was best friends, for that time, with Dena Shewchuk."

Adam tilted his head to one side, as if studying her. "How old were you then?"

"Thirteen." Her first year as a teenager. Her last as part of a complete family unit. Her parents had separated shortly after their brief stay in Derwin.

"I remember you now. You used to come to youth group with Dena."

"Youth group made a huge impact on my life," she replied, pleased that he had recognized her. "Your faith was an encouragement to me."

It was as if someone had thrown a switch. His lips thinned. His eyes narrowed. "That was a long time ago." He turned away from her and walked over to the counter.

"Now I know who you are," Helen said, tapping her cheek with her forefinger. "A lady named Visser was buried here a year ago. Any relation?"

Melanie tuned back to Helen, the mention of her mother bringing a familiar pain, softened by time.

"That was my mother. She loved Derwin as much as I did, and she wanted to be buried here."

"I'm sorry for you," Helen said.

"Thanks." An awkward silence sprang up, broken by the clink of dishes that Adam was washing up in the sink.

Tiffany's entire attention was focused on trying to pick up a couple of chocolate chips that had fallen from her cookie, but she had succeeded only in mashing one of them onto the table.

Melanie reached over and picked the other one up and handed it to her.

"Did you buy this house from the Shewchuks?" Melanie asked when Tiffany took the chip.

"No. Adam did. A number of years ago."

"They were such a happy family," Melanie said wistfully. "I never thought they would move. I always thought that part of the reason for their happiness was this house."

"The Shewchuks were not a happy family when I bought this house." Adam's derision underlined his previous withdrawal.

"Adam, you stop that right now." Helen flashed

him an admonishing look, her brief display of spunk surprising Melanie.

Adam ignored her as he carefully wiped Tiffany's hands with a wet cloth. ''Come on, Tiff, let's go back outside,'' he said, tossing the cloth into the sink and holding out his arms for his daughter.

''Don't wanna go.'' She pouted, pulling away from her father. ''Want Gramma.''

Adam gently picked her up and set her on his hip. ''Gramma is tired,'' he said, tucking a curl of hair behind his daughter's ear, his head angling to catch her eyes.

Melanie couldn't help but watch the interplay between father and daughter. Couldn't help but be touched by the tenderness Adam showed her. It called out to a basic yearning that had been growing the past few years. A yearning for a family. For a place of her own.

But Tiffany twisted away from him, turning instead to her grandmother. ''Want Gramma,'' she whined, her chubby little hands reaching out to Helen.

Once again Melanie caught the glimpse of pain in Adam's face she had seen earlier, and she wondered at the relationship between father and daughter.

''Gramma has to talk to the nurse,'' Adam said, pulling her closer. ''And we have to work some more outside.'' Adam glanced at Melanie, as if apologizing for his daughter's behavior. But as their eyes met, some indefinable emotion arced between them, caught their gazes in a gentler snare. Melanie couldn't look away.

Adam broke the connection first, turning to Tiffany, who had given up on her protest. "Let's go, honey," he said quietly, leaving the room.

Melanie glanced down at the papers, trying to compose herself. Her cherished memories were under assault. Adam. The Shewchuks.

Helen leaned over and patted her lightly on the hand. "Are you okay?"

Melanie smiled at the concern in Helen's voice. The patient asking after the nurse. "I'm fine," she said, tilting a grin at Helen. "Now, let's get you settled in your bed."

Melanie opened the door of the bedroom, and as she let Helen precede her, couldn't suppress her intake of breath. Windows, curved in a half circle in one corner, spilled a profusion of light into the room.

Though the rest of the house looked generally worn down, this room looked like a fairy tale. The walls were painted in a pale buttery yellow and soft organza scarf curtains swathed the windows. Melanie immediately recognized one corner of the room as the turret she had been so entranced with as a child.

"This is beautiful," she breathed as she followed Helen's slow progress to the large maple sleigh bed that dominated the room. A pale-yellow-and-aqua pieced quilt covered it.

"Isn't it lovely? And I made Lana and Adam the quilt as a wedding present." Helen paused, and Melanie could see the glint of tears in her eyes. "You have to excuse my son. He used to be such a happy person. But now he is so bitter. He used to go to church, but he says it's a waste of time. He says he doesn't believe in God, but I know God will still work in his life.'' Melanie could see love shining from her client's face.

Helen leaned forward, grasping Melanie's hand, her grip surprisingly strong. ''Are you a praying woman?''

Melanie smiled at her and nodded. ''I can't get through my day unless I start it with the Lord.''

''When you pray, can you remember me?'' Her gaze was earnest, her bright blue eyes piercing. ''Adam wants to move me down to Calgary to some concrete building. I don't want to go there.''

Melanie was concerned at the intensity in Helen's voice. What Adam had decided for his mother was between them. But she couldn't ignore the entreaty in Helen's face. ''I'll pray for you, Helen,'' she said, laying her hand over Helen's. It was all she could say.

Helen released her grip on Melanie's arm and slowly sagged back against the pillows. ''Thank you, Melanie. Adam is a good son—he just doesn't understand. He used to love this house. But now...he can't be here more than one day. He doesn't visit, and now he wants me to move to Calgary. I was born and raised in the country.'' Helen clutched her chest, her eyes wide. ''I can't live in the city.''

Melanie caught her by the wrist, her fingers on Helen's pulse. Elevated. She laid her hand against her burning cheek. Too warm. ''I'm going to take your temperature,'' she said. ''I'll be right back.''

Her temperature registered a couple of degrees above normal, and when Melanie checked her incision, it showed no sign of infection.

Stress most likely was the cause, she thought.

"You need to relax, Helen," Melanie said, helping her ease back onto the bed. "You just concentrate on getting better."

"Will you talk to Adam about me staying here? He can be stubborn and I don't have the strength to fight him. He says he wants to protect me, but I don't need to be protected."

Melanie nodded, albeit somewhat reluctantly.

"Will you pray for him, too? He's had a tough few years. You used to know him. I'm hoping you can help him, too."

"I'm here to take care of you, Helen," Melanie said quietly. And only you, she reminded herself.

Adam and his daughter were a burden she wasn't ready to take on. No matter how adorable the daughter, or attractive the father.

Chapter Two

～

"**N**ow it's official." Floyd gave the nail on the for-sale sign one more tap.

Adam hitched Tiffany higher up on his hip, his eyes on the bright yellow sign now firmly attached to the fence in front of the house. He pushed aside second and third thoughts.

It had been Lana's house and Lana's dream. Getting rid of this last tie to Derwin was the smart thing to do.

"Go down." Tiffany patted Adam's shoulder with a chubby hand and Adam turned back to her. Eyes as intensely blue as the Alberta sky above them stared back at him, her expression holding the same serious look it had since she was a tiny baby.

"In a minute, honey," he said softly, giving her a light squeeze. He turned his attention back to Floyd, the real estate agent. "So now what happens?"

"We've already done all the necessary paperwork, listing contract and all that. Now I start doing my job.'' Floyd set the hammer on the fence post and glanced over his shoulder at the house.

''Handyman's special,'' Floyd mused. ''Though it needs work, it has potential. It's got great lines. I love that tower.''

''Down,'' Tiffany insisted, wiggling once more in his arms.

''You can go down, but don't go into the house,'' he warned, lowering his daughter to the ground. ''Gramma is busy.'' Busy with Melanie of the amber eyes and the chocolate-brown hair.

The thought came from nowhere and he pushed it back, still surprised at his reaction to Melanie Visser. She had been quite young when she lived here, but already then her unusually colored eyes made you give her a second look. Now she had matured into a beautiful woman.

He had tried to dismiss his reaction to her, but he couldn't dismiss the fact that she was the first woman who had held any kind of appeal since Lana. He wondered if she was unattached.

The door of the house slapped shut. Footsteps echoed on the wooden porch behind them. Floyd straightened and with his thumb and forefinger tugged the lapel of his blazer, pulled back his shoulders in an unconscious preening gesture. Adam's back was to the house, but it wasn't hard for him to guess that Melanie was coming toward them.

An errant scent of soap mixed with a curious fragrance of peaches confirmed his guess.

''Good morning, ma'am,'' Floyd said, his smile holding a different line than before.

If Floyd had had a cowboy hat, Adam felt sure he would have tipped it.

Adam glanced at Melanie. "Melanie, this is Floyd Wierenga, the real estate agent. Floyd, this is Melanie Visser. The new health nurse."

Melanie gave Floyd a polite smile and shook his hand. "Nice to meet you."

"How long have you been here?" Floyd asked.

"About a month."

Floyd reached inside his coat. "Well, if you and your husband are ever in the market for a place…" He let the words drift away as he handed Melanie a card.

Melanie glanced down at it and then at the sign Floyd had just put up.

"I'm single, but I might be," she said, tapping the card on the palm of her hand.

"That's just great to hear. I know we've got a number of properties that might work out quite well for you." Floyd turned back to Adam. "Pleasure, Adam. Good to see you again." He shook Adam's hand, winked at Melanie and in a matter of moments stepped into his truck and was gone.

Melanie glanced at the card in her hand, flicking it between her fingers, then at the sign. "I'm guessing you're serious about selling the house?"

Adam gave her a puzzled look. "Are you interested?"

She chewed her lip, as if considering. "I love this place," she said softly. "Would love to live here."

"I don't know if it's suitable for a single woman, unless there's someone…" He let the question die the death it should have a few words previously. What business was it of his whether she had anyone in her life or not?

Melanie laughed lightly, unfazed by Adam's blunt question. "No, there's no one as yet. But I've dreamed about this house since the first day I saw it. I can't believe you're selling it."

"It needs a lot of work. And money."

Melanie angled him a quizzical glance. "You sound like you're trying to talk me out of it. Unless you're using reverse psychology."

"I don't work that way." Adam glanced over his shoulder. Tiffany was squatted down, quite content for the moment, her chubby hands drawing in the sand with a twig.

He turned back to Melanie, who stood with her arms clasped in front of her, looking up at the house with a dreamy smile. Why would she want this house? It would be nothing but a headache for her.

"How long have you owned it?" Melanie asked.

"I've had it for about four years. My wife and I lived in it for only one. How's my mother doing?" he asked, forestalling any more questions.

"She's resting now. She just had a bad spell."

"How bad?"

"She spiked a temp for no reason that I could see. She's okay now, though I am concerned about her blood pressure. Make sure you keep an eye on her and if you have any concerns, call me."

Adam felt icy fingers clutch his temple. Not again. "Will I need to call an ambulance?"

"I doubt it. She's not that bad," Melanie hastened to add.

"What about moving her?"

Melanie frowned at him, flicking the real estate agent's card between her fingers.

"To be honest, right now the best thing for your mother is stability. It takes about six weeks for full healing."

"That long?" Adam shook his head. "She can't be here alone six weeks, and I can't stay here that long." He had been getting ready for a long-overdue vacation with Tiffany when he got the phone call from the hospital in Derwin. He'd canceled his plans but not his time off, so that he could be here.

"It doesn't sound like she will enjoy moving back to the city. And I understand you're on holidays."

"Not even I can go on vacation for six weeks." Adam caught Melanie's smile and shook his head. "I should warn you. My mother has her own agenda. She moved out of her apartment in town and in here after our last renters moved out six months ago, hoping that would stop me from selling it." And it had. Until her accident a week ago. "She has this feeling about this house." He glanced back over his shoulder, as if his mother's emotions were creeping up on him and threatening to shove aside his well-laid plans.

"It is a lovely place. I have to agree."

"Well, for now, she's staying, but as soon as she can be moved, she will be. I'd like you to help me prepare her for that."

He didn't want to stay here any longer than necessary.

"I'll do what I can," Melanie said, tucking her hair behind her ear as she glanced up at him.

As their eyes met, he felt it again. The connection to the past. A connection that called to other times in his life and a deeper hunger that he'd ignored for a long time.

"I appreciate the help," he said, stepping back. As if he needed to create a physical space between them.

For his own sake more than anything. Right now he had enough complications in his life. He didn't need to get his emotions tangled up in a temporary situation.

"Is the asking price negotiable?"

Melanie tucked the phone under her ear as she made a quick note on a pad of paper. She had waited a day after she saw the house, trying to talk herself out of this crazy scheme, but she couldn't.

"It's going to need quite a large cash outlay if you want to finish it off," Floyd continued. "If you want, I've got a few places in town that you might be interested in."

"I could do it bit by bit." Melanie ignored his other offer and curled her bare feet around the metal legs of her kitchen chair. Bit by bit might not cut it. It would be a major project, but how wonderful it would be to see the house transformed. Loved.

"Ideally I'd like to be around to show you the property, but I can't do it until Monday."

"I'm there every day. I could have Adam show me around. Don't worry, you'll still get your commission."

"Of course I will. The agreement I got Adam to sign is ironclad. He can't back out if I have a buyer," Floyd said with a laugh. "Phone me after you've seen it, then, and we can go from there."

As Melanie hung up the phone, she sat back in her kitchen chair. In comparison to the lovely open spaces of the house, her apartment felt cramped, and instead of trees and a large yard, she overlooked a parking lot. Just like all the other apartments she and her family had lived in, dragged around the country by a father always on the move. Always on the lookout for a chance to make more money doing less work.

By the time they had moved to Derwin, she had been through six schools in seven years.

Harold Visser had promised Melanie and her mother that he was going to settle down in Derwin. Buy a house. Make a home. Go to church with Melanie and her mother.

Though they'd stayed in Derwin longer than most places, in fourteen months they'd been on the move again. But this time her parents had separated and Melanie and her mother had gone their own way.

When Melanie had graduated from high school, she'd become a nurse. She had lived in more small apartments, saving every penny for a place of her own. Thanks to a legacy left her when her father died and thanks to her own scrimping and saving, she now had a sizable down payment for a house.

Melanie fought a pang of sorrow as she doodled an elaborate circle around the Engler house price she had scribbled down. Her dream was supposed to have included her mother. But now Melanie lived on her own, and more than ever she yearned for a permanent place. A home.

And as Melanie opened her Bible later that night, she searched for familiar passages of comfort. She turned to Psalms and read in Psalm 84, "Even the sparrow has found a home, and the swallow a nest for herself, where she may have her young, a place near your altar." Melanie put her finger on the passage and read it again.

Home. It was what she had wanted ever since she had got to know Dena Shewchuk. She had dreamed about owning a home, a place that stayed the same. Even sparrows and swallows look for and desire a home.

Melanie finished reading, then snapped off the light of her bedside table and snuggled into her blankets. She thought again of the house. It was like a dream to think that the one place that represented all she longed for might be hers. If she was willing to make the commitment. And she was. She had a good job now. Though classified as part-time, she was working full-time hours with the promise that it would be turned into a permanent job.

Everything was in place. But if she bought the house, what would happen to Helen?

That thought stopped her. Helen would need another place to live. And if Adam was willing to offer her that, it shouldn't be Melanie's concern.

I want to help them, Lord, she prayed, looking out the window of her apartment into the small sliver of the evening sky that she could see out her window. *Give me the wisdom I need to do it.*

She rolled over and pulled her blankets up around her shoulder. And as she drifted off to sleep, her last thoughts were of wavy hair and blue eyes.

Adam stripped his leather gloves off and sauntered up to the house, mentally noting the work he still had to do before this yard was cleared off.

Piles of lumber draped with tarps covered part of the yard close to the house. Bricks, once neatly stacked up, now lay tumbled beside the lumber. The lumber was for the rooms he had been going to put in the basement. The brick for the fireplace that Lana had wanted rebuilt.

The clench of sorrow he felt was unexpected and unwelcome. He should be over Lana's death by now. At least, that's what the grief counselor had said.

It was this house, he thought as he jogged up the back steps and yanked open the screen door to the porch. Each time he turned around he was faced with memories of Lana.

The memories not only hurt, they accused.

"Is that you, Melanie?" he heard his mother call from her bedroom.

"Sorry to disappoint you, Mom," Adam called back, washing his hands. "It's just me."

Helen lay in her bed, her hands folded over her chest, her features drawn. Tiffany lay on the floor beside her, coloring with some fat crayons that Adam had bought for her in town yesterday.

"Are you going to make some coffee for Melanie?"

"In a minute." Adam threw the towel into the

laundry basket in the corner of his mother's bedroom and carefully lowered himself onto the edge of her bed. "Do you want to stay in bed this morning?"

"I'd like to, but I'm sure Melanie will get me up when she gets here." She sighed lightly, fingering a fold in the quilt. "Adam, I know you don't like being here. But I still think it's the best place for you and your little girl. You have to think of Tiffany, as well."

"I do, Mother," he said with a forced smile. "I think of her needs all the time."

"But Lana's family…"

"They can come and see her any time now. Eastbar is only half an hour away. Calgary a couple of hours." Adam saw a flash of reflected light through the far window and got up. Through the fly-specked glass he saw a small red car come to a halt in front of the house, and Melanie got out.

In spite of the sorrow he had felt only moments ago, Adam felt a stir of reaction. Even stronger than the one he'd felt when he met her yesterday.

Today her hair swung to her shoulders, catching the sun like melted chocolate. Her loose pants, tied low on her hips, and her flowing cotton shirt couldn't hide the easy grace of her slender limbs.

Beautiful, he thought, watching as she stopped, looking up at the house. A faint smile played on her lips.

What was she thinking about? What was going on behind those unique amber eyes?

He turned away from the window to catch his mother grinning at him, looking livelier than she had a few moments ago. "Lovely girl, isn't she?"

Adam didn't even acknowledge her comment. "Do you still want to wait here for her, or do you want to go to the kitchen?"

"I'll wait here."

"Suit yourself." He crouched down beside Tiffany and fingered a curl away from her face. "Are you coming with me, punkin, or are you going to stay with Gramma?"

"Stay with Gramma," Tiffany replied, not even looking up.

Tiffany's devotion to a grandmother she hardly knew surprised him. Since they had come back to Derwin a week ago, it was as if Tiffany had forged a unique bond with her. His daughter still acted reserved around him and it still hurt. A lot.

He closed the door to the bedroom and went to open the door for Melanie.

She stood on the step, looking over the yard beside the house, her fingers resting lightly on the railing of the veranda.

As he watched, she leaned forward, looking around the yard, her eyes bright, her mouth lifted in a large smile of pure pleasure. And he wondered what caused it.

He opened the door. "Good morning, Melanie."

Melanie jumped, looking guilty.

"Sorry. I was just looking at the yard. It's so lovely."

"You must have a good imagination to be able to see past the piles of lumber."

Melanie just smiled. "I remember it from before."

"So you said. How many years ago was that?"

"Probably about fourteen. I've always loved this place." She glanced back at him over her shoulder. "I phoned your real estate agent last night. I thought I would let you know I'm serious about buying the house."

Adam leaned against the door frame, surprised that his disparaging comments from the day before hadn't deterred her.

"Floyd told you my asking price?"

"He did, and I was hoping, if you had time, that you could show me around the house after I'm done with your mother."

"I can't talk you out of it, can I?"

Melanie frowned. "You're the worst salesperson. No. I love this place and I'd like a tour."

Adam was just going to consent and then look away, the picture of casual, when something in her eyes drew his, held them.

What was it about her that caused this lapse? This appeal that he wished wasn't there? In the past three years he had neither been given nor taken the opportunity to spend any kind of time with another woman. He was a widower with a little girl who needed him.

And now his mother needed him. He didn't have time for any kind of flirtation, casual or otherwise.

Melanie smiled up at him, and in spite of his previous rationalizing, for the first time in years he felt an answering lift in his chest. A lightness in his mind.

"Is your mother inside?"

Adam pulled himself together. Gathered his wandering emotions. "Yes. She's in her bedroom."

"Then I'll see you later?" She turned the statement into a question.

"Yeah. I'll be out back." He held the door open for her, and just before she stepped through, she gave him another glance. Another smile.

And Adam's heart gave another lift.

Chapter Three

Melanie lowered Tiffany to her bed and gently tucked the quilt under her chin. Tiffany stiffened, then settled down, her eyelids flickering.

Melanie smoothed down a tuft of hair. She remembered putting Dena's little brother to bed in this same room when she and Dena would baby-sit. She could recall so easily the soft, heavy warmth of a sleeping child. Dena had always complained, but as an only child Melanie had loved the responsibility of younger brothers and sisters and the squabbling and laughter that would ebb and flow through the house.

She closed the door behind her with a soft click and walked quietly down the hallway. Her fingers trailed the banister once worn smooth from bodies sliding down it, now sticky with accumulated grime.

She stopped at the bottom of the stairs, listening. She could almost hear the sound of Dena's father's booming voice as he came home from work. The squeal of children all running to be the first to greet him.

Now the house lay quiet, slumbering in the early afternoon. Sun flowed into the kitchen, showing— more vividly than Adam's words could—the neglect of the house.

This house needed a family who cared, Melanie thought, her memories superimposing themselves on the scene.

You're not a family.

The words echoed through a life as empty as this house, mocking her decision. What's a single girl like you doing thinking of buying a house?

Someday she had hoped she would meet someone with whom she could share her life, but her mother's experience had made her cautious.

In the meantime she wasn't going to sit around and wait for the knight she and Dena had dreamed of. She meant to take charge of her own life. And if that meant buying a house as a single girl, then so be it.

She stepped out onto the porch and saw Adam.

He was piling lumber onto a trailer behind his half-ton truck. Melanie knew she should let him know she was there, but her memories kept her in the shadows of the porch, watching.

His back glistened, his muscles working as he picked up another load of wood. His hair, damp from sweat, curled around his face, softening the hard lines.

A faint echo of the yearning she had felt tucking Tiffany in struck her again. But she stopped herself.

He's not the hero from your past, Melanie reminded herself. She knew what she wanted in life.

Knew what she wanted in a future partner. Adam was not it, she thought, remembering what Helen had said about Adam giving up on God.

So why did she still feel this strange connection with him?

She cleared her throat, and Adam looked up.

"I was wondering if you had the time to show me around?"

He grabbed his shirt hanging over the side of his truck. As he threaded his arms through the sleeves he called out, "Just give me a chance to check on my daughter…."

"She's sleeping."

Adam's fingers paused over the snaps. "Sleeping? In my mother's room?"

"No. I laid her down in what I presumed was her bedroom. I took a wild guess and figured that she would be the only one who had a quilt covered with cartoon ducks."

"You didn't have to do that," he said, his tone defensive as he came closer.

"Probably not," Melanie admitted, with an attempt at humor and a smile. "But I didn't think she'd appreciate the crick she would get in her neck from lying all twisted on your mother's bedroom floor."

She was rewarded with an absent nod from Adam as he rolled up the cuffs of his shirt. "Where did you want to start?"

"Well, I've already seen your mother's room and…"

"Actually, that's the master bedroom. It was the

first room that I fixed up. It needed some structural work, but my wife wanted at least one room done.''

His wife. Lana.

''Why don't you surprise me?'' she said.

''Not my specialty, I'm afraid,'' he returned, a ghost of a smile glimmering over his lips.

A smile that did funny things to her heart.

''Well, let's start with the basics,'' she said brusquely, masking her reaction to him.

Melanie didn't know much about houses, or buildings or construction work, but Adam did. As she requested, he took her down to the basement.

''The foundation is solid, but some of the floor joists need to be replaced.'' Adam pointed out which ones, pursing his lips.

''Is that a lot of work?''

''Most definitely. And costly.''

''Can you tell me how much?''

''Not offhand, but if you want I can break down some of the expenses.''

She nodded, as second thoughts began nibbling at her confidence.

''You're going to need to install a new hot water tank. This one is rusted and will probably not pass the house inspection.'' Adam gestured toward a large squat tank perched in the corner. She and Dena used to hide behind it and scare her brothers and sisters when they would come down to the cold room on some errand for their mother.

''The furnace is not too bad. But same thing again. It's old and will some day need to be replaced. The newer ones are much quieter.''

"It always made such a huge rumble when it started up in the morning," Melanie said with a smile. "It sounded like a plane taking off. You could hear it all the way upstairs."

"Well, that rumble is not what you want to hear." He showed her the cold room, with its familiar musty smell still permeating the wood. It, too, needed work.

"The wiring at least is up to code now," he said, letting her precede him up the stairs to the kitchen. "I had to install a larger breaker box to carry the extra wiring I wanted to do in here. There aren't near enough electrical outlets. Especially in the kitchen and the bedrooms."

"I know. The Shewchuks used to have extension cords all over the place."

"They're lucky they didn't have a fire," Adam said as he held open the door at the top of the stairs. "When I bought the house from them, every outlet was doubled and tripled up. Not a good thing."

Adam stopped in the middle of the kitchen, his hands on his hips as he drew in a sigh. "Now, this is one room I was itching to redo. Those cabinets are simply awful."

"I like the design," Melanie said with a smile. "Turn of the century, aren't they? A fresh coat of paint would make them look better."

"It won't make them work better. They're all out of whack. None of the doors are plumb and most of the drawers stick."

Melanie didn't respond to his negative comment. Instead she walked over to the bay window and sank onto the seat built into it. "I have always loved this spot. We used to sit here and read and eat apples. Mrs. Shewchuk would be busy in the kitchen, baking and cooking and making our mouths water with all the lovely smells.'' She laughed lightly, turning to look at the rest of the kitchen.

Adam shook his head as if in disbelief. ''You're bound and determined to see past the work this house needs, aren't you?''

Melanie dismissed his comment with a wave of her hand. ''And you're bound and determined to show the worst side of this house. If Floyd knew how you were talking, he'd have a fit.''

Adam snorted. ''Real estate agents have their own language. I speak plain English.''

''But it is a beautiful house, don't you think? You must have thought so at one time or you wouldn't have bought it.''

Adam only shrugged. ''The reality is, this house needs a lot of work. I would be lying if I didn't tell you that. The eaves and soffits need to be repainted. The attic needs a new vent. I could go on.''

''You know quite a bit about building.'' Melanie wanted to stop the list of all the work that needed to be done. He was giving her second thoughts and she didn't want to allow them entrance. For the first time in her life, she felt as if she had found a home.

''I should. I'm a general contractor.''

''So you work for yourself?''

He nodded.

''How did you manage to take time off for your mother?''

''I'm technically on my holidays.'' He glanced

around the room with a faint grimace. "Tiffany and I were going to go to Disneyland."

Melanie stifled a shudder. She couldn't imagine how a child as young as Tiffany would enjoy being dragged around a venue as busy as Disneyland. "I think this is a better alternative," she said. "She has a lovely yard to play in. She has time to connect with you and her grandmother."

Adam only shrugged. Melanie figured she had already said too much, so she might as well press her next point.

"I have to confess, besides you showing me the house, I want to talk to you about your mother." *Please Lord, give me the right words,* she prayed. "I know you asked me to help you out. Help her get used to the idea about moving. But she got quite upset when I mentioned it just now. She was running a fever."

Adam angled her a puzzled glance. "How do you make the connection between her fever and my moving? It's probably from her surgery."

Melanie shook her head. "The wound is clean with no sign of infection. She had a temp yesterday, as well. Strange as it sounds, it isn't unusual for this to happen. For stress to bring on a temperature." She folded her arms over her chest, striving to look professional and in charge. She knew Adam wouldn't like what she had to say next. "I think you should reconsider moving her so soon."

Adam shook his head. "And how am I supposed to do that? If the house sells, I'm hooped. I've got a sick mother and then I'm pressuring her to move. Not a situation I want to put her in either.''

Melanie could see the sense in it and ventured her next suggestion. ''I'm going to be putting a firm offer on the house to Floyd, and I'm willing to wait.'' Saying the words aloud made them more real and a little more frightening. In spite of what Adam had told her, she knew deep within her being that she wanted this house.

''She so obviously wants to stay here,'' Melanie continued, sensing he was giving in. ''And it is such a good place. It's quiet, it's familiar.'' Melanie looked around the kitchen. Sure, it needed some work, but it was so homey and comfortable. How come Adam couldn't see that? ''I think she'll heal better here, in a place she's comfortable.'' She pressed her lips together for fear her next words would spill out.

And it would be a good time for you to connect with your daughter.

Adam sighed, shoving his hands through his hair, biting his lip. He did not look pleased and she felt as if she had let him down.

A faint beeping sound broke the silence and she glanced down at the pager hooked to her belt.

''Whoops. Got a message.'' They were in the kitchen, and thankfully her briefcase and nurse's bag were on the chair where she had left them.

She pulled out her cell phone, dialed the number and was put through to her supervisor. She was asked to cover for another nurse who had called in sick. Her afternoon just got busier, she thought, snapping her phone shut.

She glanced at Adam. "I have to go. The rest of the tour will have to wait until Monday when I'll be seeing your mother again," she said with a touch of regret, slinging the strap of her briefcase over her shoulder.

"Okay." Adam stepped back, slipping his hands into the back pockets of his pants. "What about getting the doctor's approval to move my mother?"

Melanie clutched the handle of her briefcase. "You don't have to take my advice, Adam," she said quietly. "If you can arrange for a stretcher and an ambulance and are willing to pay for that, you can move her any time you want. I'm just telling you what I believe is best for her in my capacity as her nurse. And I'm telling you because I know you care about her and her well-being. After all, that's the main priority here, isn't it?"

Adam held her gaze, then glanced around the room, as if looking for something. Answers, maybe.

"I'll think about it," he said.

Melanie couldn't help but feel a touch of sorrow for Helen, and for Adam, as well. She held his narrowed gaze and slowly nodded her head. It was all she could ask him to do.

As she drove away, she glanced in her rearview mirror.

Adam stood on the porch, watching her. Then the trees hid him from view, swaying lightly in the afternoon breeze.

Once again she wondered why he would want to leave this beautiful place.

* * *

"Did he say how extensive the reconstruction would be?" Bob Tessier smiled across the office table at Melanie. For the past twenty minutes she had been talking to Bob, the loans officer at her bank, and she still didn't know if the bank would be willing to lend her the money. But after seeing only part of the house yesterday she knew she wanted to buy it.

"We didn't make it to the second floor and the attic, so I'm not sure what needs to be done there."

Bob Tessier doodled on the notepad, frowning. "I know the bank would like to have an itemized account of the refurbishments necessary so we can better ascertain the value of the house."

Melanie resisted the urge to roll her eyes. The man was in sore need of a thesaurus. "I have a large down payment, which, by the way, is sitting in a bank account here. I have more than enough room to fix the house."

"That is correct. However, we need to secure our portion of the debt. And, I might remind you, your position of employment is, at best, tenuous."

"A position that will be turning into a full-time one after a meeting of the next Health Authority." Melanie smiled to overcome her growing frustration. She didn't tell him she had to apply for it, but her supervisor had practically guaranteed her the job. "But if this bank isn't willing to work with me on this, I can easily set up an appointment with someone at the credit union down the street."

Bob straightened, the implied threat changing his demeanor. "There's no need to do that, Melanie. I'm sure we can accommodate you. However, you must understand that we need to protect our investment. And I wouldn't be doing my job if I didn't advise you as to all the risks inherent in this purchase.''

Melanie didn't feel like arguing with him. Nor, in spite of her threat, did she feel like moving her account. It had taken her a couple of days just to move everything to this bank, order checks, set up her charge cards. Besides, if she did that, Bob Tessier would be hounding her every choir practice they attended together to move her account back, just as he had hounded her to bring it to their bank in the first place.

''So if you would be willing to supply a list of the necessary repairs, I will see that your loan application is expedited.'' Bob gave her a conciliatory smile. ''I have no doubt it will be approved.''

Relief tingled through Melanie. Relief mixed with a few more second thoughts based on Bob's obvious reluctance to lend her the money on this project. Buying a house as a single woman was quite a commitment. Buying a house that needed so much work might be one of the more foolish things she had done. Was she sure she wanted to do it?

She thought again of the house, the setting, the peace she felt there. She thought of her apartment. The constant moving.

She thought of her mother and how she had yearned for a place with roots. A place like Derwin, she had often said with a weary sigh.

Yes, she was sure.

''Okay. I can get Adam to draw that up.''

Bob frowned. ''He's the vendor, is he not?''

"That's correct. But he's also a general contractor."

"I'm a little concerned that his appraisal might not be without prejudice."

Melanie almost laughed. Bob should have heard Adam giving her the tour. If anything, Adam might be prejudiced against the house. "Then get a building inspector to verify." Melanie smiled past her frustration.

"I will agree to that. Once I receive that information we can proceed from there."

"I'll try to get the list to you as soon as possible." Melanie got to her feet and shook Bob's hand. "I'll be in touch."

"Looking forward to it." Bob smiled, still holding her hand, and Melanie carefully smiled back, wondering when it would be polite to reclaim her hand. She wasn't blind. Since she'd joined the choir she had been getting fairly blatant signals from him. Not that she was the least bit interested. But right now she couldn't afford to antagonize him.

"And I imagine we'll be seeing you at choir practice?" he said, coming around the desk to stand by her.

Melanie gave him a vague movement of her shoulders that she hoped wouldn't encourage him without looking rude. "Of course. I go every week." She smiled, then turned to open the door, but Bob already had it open.

"Thanks," she murmured as she walked through the door, her head bent. She was afraid to make eye contact for fear he might follow her out of the room and through the main lobby.

Bob was a good man and a kind man. He had a wonderful baritone voice. He attended the same church she did. And he was single.

None of which made any dent in her feelings for him.

She laughed at herself as she walked out of the bank and into a beautiful summer day in downtown Derwin. She was still possessed of that same silly romantic notion she had created when she and Dena would play in the top floor of the tower of the house.

While Dena's dreams were of some more modern man, Melanie's tended to be more romantic. And her hero was a knight who would come riding up on a horse. A knight worthy of her love and affection.

"Hello, Melanie."

The deep voice behind her sprang into her day-dreams. Melanie jumped and turned around, her hand on her chest.

"Sorry," Adam said with a half smile. "Didn't mean to scare you."

He was carrying his daughter easily with one arm, his other hand hooked into a couple of plastic bags. "You were certainly lost in thought. I called you a couple of times."

Melanie looked up into his blue, blue eyes, blinked, then looked away. Having her hand held by Bob Tessier didn't even come close to the impact this man's gaze had on her.

"Sorry, I was just at the bank." Her hand fluttered

in the direction of the building behind him. "I was talking to them about the house, actually."

"Really?" Adam shifted Tiffany's weight on his arm.

"Do you want me to take her?" Melanie said, holding out her hands. "You look like you have enough to carry."

"No, that's okay." Adam smiled at Tiffany, giving her a light hitch. "She's not heavy." He spoke with such pride and love that Melanie felt an echo of the yearning she had had a couple of days ago. Had her father ever looked at her with such longing? Such pride?

Tiffany was a lucky little girl.

"Want to go." Tiffany leaned toward Melanie and away from Adam.

Pain flickered in Adam's eyes, deepened the frown on his forehead, and Melanie regretted making the offer.

But Tiffany's forward momentum made it awkward for him to continue holding her, so Melanie lifted her hands higher and took Tiffany out of his arms.

"Actually, it's good I met you. I need to talk to you about the house," Melanie continued, pulling Tiffany close to her as she tried to fill the uneasy silence that followed. They came to the corner of the main street. Across from them was the park, its tall trees and soft grass beckoning.

"We can sit there while we talk," Adam said. "Tiffany could use a break from cement sidewalks and stores. But I don't want to leave my mom alone too long."

His devotion to his mother and his daughter was heartwarming. She couldn't help but think of her father, whose contact with her before he died had been minimal at best.

"It won't take long."

As soon as they got to the park Melanie crouched to set Tiffany down, but she clung to Melanie's neck. "Stay with you," she demanded, her fingers tangling in Melanie's hair.

Adam set the grocery bags on the ground and sat beside her, his knees resting on his elbows. He angled her an aggrieved look, which she guessed had much to do with the fact that Tiffany was on her lap and not his. When his eyes flicked to his daughter, Melanie knew it to be true.

He looked down at his hands, pressing his thumbs against each other. "So what exactly did you need to know?"

"Bob Tessier at the bank wants you to make a list of all the repairs that the house needs done and a possible estimate of the cost."

"Are you sure you want me to do this?"

Melanie lifted her shoulder in a shrug. "You seem to know best what needs to be done. I assured Bob you would be impartial."

"I'll have to write that down to remind me." He pulled a pen out of his pocket, clicked it and scribbled the information on the back of his hand.

"Do you know how bad that ink is for you?"

Adam shrugged. "That's some old wives' tale. I'm surprised a professional like you would bother to repeat it.'' He smiled at her again, the faint outline of a dimple appearing in his cheek.

''There's been countless studies done on it,'' she said, trying to keep her expression stern. ''You'll be sorry when you're on your deathbed, dying of some ink-related illness, that you didn't listen to me.''

''I might, at that,'' he said quietly.

''Listen? To you?'' Tiffany repeated, catching Melanie's face in her hands as if not appreciating being left out of the conversation. Melanie turned to her, smiling at the little girl's serious expression.

''I'm just talking to your daddy.'' Melanie touched her nose to the little girl's and was rewarded with a bright smile. ''Do you want to sit with your daddy?''

Tiffany looked over at Adam, who had straightened as if waiting, and Melanie realized what a tenuous situation she had created with her thoughtless question. Thankfully Tiffany got down and toddled over to her father.

''So you're thinking of buying the house.'' Adam pulled Tiffany up on his lap. ''Why?''

How to explain the emotions the house engendered. The feeling that given the proper care, the house could be a home that welcomed people. ''I've always been in love with that house,'' she said, realizing how silly it might sound. ''I think it could be a good investment, once it's fixed up.''

''But a single woman like you. Surely you don't need the headache.''

''I don't think it would be a headache,'' she said quietly. ''I think it would be wonderful to have a home.''

Adam's laugh was a harsh sound. "Trust me, Melanie, that house is no home."

The sharp sound of his reply pulled her out of her reverie. "Why do you say that?"

Adam didn't reply. Simply toyed with his daughter's hair.

"Is it because of your wife?"

His scowl showed her that she had hit a bull's-eye. And a sensitive point. "Maybe" was all he said.

She wanted to know more and was wondering how to ask him when a young woman called out his name and came running toward them, shattering the moment.

"I heard you were back in town." She stopped in front of Adam, smiling broadly. Her blond hair was pulled up in a loose twist, strands artfully framing her face. Her sleeveless shirt barely skimmed the waistband of her low-cut blue jeans. Melanie caught the glimmer of a ring in her navel.

"Hello, Roxanne." Adam politely stood up, still holding Tiffany like a shield.

"It's been ages since you've been around," she said, disregarding his retreat. She slipped an arm around his waist.

Adam threw Melanie an aggrieved glance over Tiffany's head and patted Roxanne awkwardly on her shoulder with his one free hand.

Roxanne pulled back. "The Gerrard family has been asking about you. Wondering when you were going to come around with Tiffany." Roxanne stroked the little girl's cheek, but Tiffany pulled away.

Adam said nothing, his eyes narrowing, his lips thinning. Melanie had heard bits and pieces from the girls at work about the Gerrards, Lana's family. They lived in Eastbar, not far from here.

"They know where I'm staying. They can come around any time."

"I'll tell them next time I see them." Roxanne turned to Melanie as if trying to fit her in the picture.

Adam introduced her, and Roxanne merely nodded, dismissing her with that one curt movement. But as their eyes met, Melanie felt a twinge of recognition.

Roxanne must have felt it, too. "Do I know you?" she asked.

"Melanie used to live in Derwin. About fourteen years ago," Adam offered.

Roxanne straightened, looking from Adam to Melanie. Time hovered and a vague memory coalesced.

Melanie was a young girl again. New to the school. Coming in halfway through the grade eight school year. She was pushed up against the wall of the school, being teased about her clothes, her hair and her makeup by two young girls. One of them was Roxanne.

Melanie was frightened and crying, something the girls thought quite funny.

Then a tall young man came by. He stopped, looked the situation over and, though he didn't know Melanie nor she him, he held out his hand to her.

"Hey, there," he said with a smile and a dimple. "I've been looking for you."

The girls stepped back. Roxanne's mouth fell open as she looked from Melanie to the young man.

And Melanie took his hand and walked away with him.

It was a crazy chance she'd taken then, Melanie realized. She had known nothing about him. Yet at that moment she'd been convinced this young man would not hurt her. That she was safe with him.

That young man was, of course, Adam.

"Don't remember," Roxanne said, dismissing her. She turned back to Adam. "So you going to go to the community barbecue? I think some of the Gerrards are going to be there."

"I might be in Calgary by then," Adam said, holding Tiffany with both arms, forestalling any more shows of affection by Roxanne.

"Well, if you're still around, come on by." Unfazed by Adam's body language, she laid a hand on his arm. "It's so good to see you back. Don't be such a stranger." She turned to Melanie and gave her a vague "See you around." Tiffany got a pat on the head, and with one last teasing smile at Adam, Roxanne was gone.

Melanie felt a little breathless, both with the energy Roxanne exuded and the memory.

Her knight in shining armor.

Melanie pushed the thought aside. Adam was no knight. He was a widower with enough on his mind.

And she was in the process of buying the house he wanted to sell so he could move to the city.

"Did you need to know anything more from me?" Adam asked, turning to her.

Melanie shook her head. "I have tomorrow off. It's Saturday, but I'd like to come by and see your mother anyhow. Maybe I could get you to finish our tour of the house then?"

"I can do that."

"Go see her." Tiffany pointed to Melanie. Adam obliged, setting his daughter down.

As Tiffany toddled over to Melanie, Adam sat down and pushed his hair back from his face with a sigh. "I wish I knew why she did this," he said softly. He raised his head to Melanie, his hands dangling between his knees. "She seems to prefer any stranger to me."

His pained expression created a responding tug. She had a good idea why Tiffany treated him the way she did, but this time she was going to be a bit more careful about speaking her mind. "She didn't prefer Roxanne."

Adam lifted one shoulder in a shrug. "That's true enough."

"Besides, she might be the kind of child who goes easily to others," Melanie said, choosing her words with care. "I've seen it happen many times." That was true. Some children went easily to strangers. Were only too happy to spend time with other adults. Others made strange at the slightest notice from any other adult. Tiffany was obviously the former.

"Who knows?" he said, rubbing his chin with his finger. "C'mon, baby, time to go."

Once again Tiffany returned willingly to his arms, creating a smile on her father's lips. Adam hefted Tiffany to his hip, then snapped his fingers. "I almost forgot. I was supposed to ask you to come for supper tomorrow night. I tried to phone you, but there was no answer.'' He took the bags from her, their fingers tangling in the plastic handles. ''Just so you're warned, I'm cooking, so you can turn down the invite and my feelings won't be hurt.''

Melanie sensed Adam's reluctance at having her visit. She knew he didn't quite trust her assessment of his mother and her care. But the thought of sitting at home alone on a Saturday night was just too forlorn.

''I don't mind finding out what your cooking is like,'' she said quietly. ''Besides, I'd like to see the rest of the house.''

''Then we'll see you tomorrow night.''

Melanie nodded. The idea was more appealing than she liked to admit.

Chapter Four

"That was very delicious, Adam." Melanie wiped her mouth and set her napkin beside her plate.

"I'm glad you enjoyed it." Adam had to admit he was quite pleased with his efforts. "I did take a cooking class so I would at least know the difference between a pot and a pan."

"Vital information, indeed," Melanie murmured with a sparkle in her eye.

Again Adam found himself looking at her, holding her gaze, reconciling the young girl he remembered with this very attractive young woman who wasn't scared to speak her mind. And whether he liked to admit it or not, something elemental was happening between them. Feelings he really didn't have time or space for in his life. Feelings he wanted to deny because they seemed disloyal to Lana's memory.

"I have to say myself, it was excellent, Adam," Helen said as well. Adam glanced his mother's way, his cheeks warming as he caught the wink she gave him. His mother had been at him all day about Melanie, how wonderful she was with Tiffany, how caring and considerate she was. And a good Christian girl.

Not that it mattered, Adam thought, folding up his napkin. He wasn't looking.

"Get down," Tiffany said, pushing herself back from the table.

"You need to go to bed, sweetheart," Adam said, picking her up. She leaned back in his arms, her blue eyes wide as she stared at him as she would a total stranger.

She did that just often enough to remind him she wasn't sure of him. Which always hit him right in the guilt zone.

Once things slowed down with the business, he would be home more, he reminded himself as he walked up the stairs to her bedroom. He just didn't have time right now.

He took his time tucking her in. Playing with her. By the time he left, she was smiling, curled up in her bed, her teddy bear tucked under one chubby arm. He turned at the doorway, looking back at her, the light from the hallway slanting into her room. He couldn't help but wonder what his life would have been like had Lana lived and they had stayed here, in this house, as a family.

It hadn't happened that way, he thought with a trace of bitterness. That was over. He closed the door and trudged toward the stairs. As he walked down the hallway to the kitchen, he heard Melanie's laughter, Helen's responding chuckle.

Melanie had already cleared the table and was washing the dishes, an old apron of his mother's tied over her dress, a tea towel slung over her shoulder. She was wearing a simple sheath splashed with brightly colored flowers. She had put her hair up in a loose topknot, emphasizing her high cheekbones, her mysterious eyes. His mother was sitting in her chair, her cheeks flushed, her eyes bright.

"So then he told me I didn't need to bother coming around with my needles and my advice. Then he turned on the television full blast and I couldn't say anything anymore." Melanie flashed a grin at his mother. "Which is a real punishment for someone like me."

Helen laughed again. "He's a funny old coot."

"I think his problem is worse than simply Alzheimer's, which is bad enough."

"Thank the Lord my mind is good," Helen said.

Melanie glanced over her shoulder at Helen. "And my mind works like lightning. One brilliant flash and then it's gone."

Adam couldn't help but smile as Helen's laugh reverberated through the kitchen. Adam hadn't seen Helen this animated in a long time.

He leaned on the doorjamb, watching, content to simply enjoy the sight of a young, attractive woman in the kitchen of his house. The whole room seemed brighter because Melanie was there. She'd always had that effect, he realized. Even as a young girl she'd had a guileless air about her mingled with an unabashed enjoyment of life. Though he'd been older, she'd still caught his attention.

"Hey, son, if you wait any longer, Melanie will have the dishes done."

Adam felt a little sheepish at being caught staring, and pushed himself away from the door frame. He caught a towel from the bar across the stove and strode to Melanie's side at the counter.

"I guess the least I could do is dry," he said, plucking a dripping plate from the drying rack on the counter.

"I hope a dishwasher is part of your renovation plans?" Melanie asked, dropping a handful of utensils on the rack with a metallic clatter.

"Absolutely. I figure there's better things to keep a person busy."

"So, Melanie, what keeps you busy?" Helen asked. "Do you ever go out? I can't see that a beautiful girl like you spends much time alone."

Adam was about to give his mother a warning look when Melanie replied, apparently not the least put out by his mother's nosiness.

"Sometimes I work late, updating client files." Melanie dropped a dripping dish on the dish rack. "As for my social life, there's a community barbecue next weekend. I'm looking forward to that."

"You should go, too, Adam."

This time he gave his mother a pointed look.

"You don't get out enough, Adam," she said with a sweet smile, ignoring his frown. "I'm sure Melanie wouldn't mind if you came along."

A heavy silence greeted that remark. Melanie

thankfully said nothing, didn't even blink as she continued washing up.

"I can tell you what I wouldn't mind knowing," Melanie said, glancing sidelong at him, "is a decent place to get my car's oil changed."

Adam felt like hugging her. Diplomatic and unfazed by his mother's pitifully obvious matchmaking. "Try Kestrals. They were pretty good last I used them."

"Thanks for the tip." She flashed him a bright smile. "There's nothing a single woman needs more than a good mechanic."

Adam couldn't stop his answering smile. Couldn't stop himself from once again getting drawn into her infectious humor and her easy manner.

"Well, that's the last one." Melanie set a pot on the drying rack, pulled the drain and rinsed the sink out with quick, efficient movements. She turned to Helen. "I should get you to bed and then be going."

Adam felt a tug of regret at the thought of her leaving so soon. "Didn't you want to see the rest of the house?" he asked before he had a chance to think about what he was getting into.

Melanie met his gaze, her features softening. "If that's okay with you, I'd love to. I almost forgot."

He hadn't. In spite of his mixed feelings, his plans, the direction he was pushing his life in, he still found himself looking forward to her company.

He knew it was simple loneliness. An excuse to spend some time with an attractive and interesting woman. Someone from a happier, more innocent time in his life.

* * *

"And this, of course, is the top tower room. Or more accurately, turret," Adam said, opening the doorway to the room in the corner of the upstairs.

He stood aside, and Melanie had to walk past him to get into the room. Her arm brushed his, and the faintest suggestion of his aftershave teased her nostrils.

A distinctly masculine scent, she thought with a pulse of expectation. She moved farther into the room, the light from the hallway throwing an oblong of gold into the room. Dusk had fallen, though she could still see the outlines of the trees outside and the shimmer of the pond.

She walked to the curved windows as fresh memories assailed her.

"This room could use some work, too," Adam said, leaving the door open. "It needs a new light bulb."

"You better change it before your mother decides to," Melanie said, glancing over her shoulder. Adam stood silhouetted in the doorway. She couldn't read his expression, but to her surprise she heard a light chuckle.

"My mother has always had a stubborn streak," he said softly, coming to stand behind her. "And an appalling habit of sticking her nose in other people's business. I apologize for her comments downstairs."

Melanie laughed. "Don't worry. I could tell you worse stories about clients who have a brother or nephew or son who would be just perfect for me." She gave him another quick smile, hoping to ease his obvious discomfort. "But if you want to come to the barbecue, you're more than welcome."

"Thanks for the invite," he said, returning her grin. "If I'm around, I just might take you up on it."

Melanie turned back to the window. "I remember coming here with Dena. We would dress up in her mother's clothes and pretend we were noble ladies waiting for our knights to come and rescue us."

"Rescue you from what?" Melanie could hear a faint note of amusement in his voice.

"Her little brothers," Melanie said with a light laugh. "They would always interrupt our fantasy by throwing lumps of dirt up at the window. We got even, though. We brought up a bunch of balloons that were left over from one of her brothers' parties and filled them with water." She laughed. "They made a lovely splat from two stories up."

"And now?" Adam asked, his voice holding a quiet warmth. "What do you daydream about now?"

A home. A family. A place where I belong. But Adam was not the man to whom she could voice these yearnings aloud. Not anymore.

"Low interest rates and good gas mileage," she said, trying to dispel her awareness of him with light words.

"Lofty ideals," he said, his voice a soft rumble behind her.

"Set attainable goals, my mother always said."

"Your mother was a wise person."

Her mother was a lot of things, Melanie thought as other, sadder memories drifted into the evening. She, too, had loved this house. And she would have loved nothing more than to help Melanie paint and plan and fix.

She missed her mother.

She moved away from Adam closer to the window and pressed her thumb against the latch. To her surprise it opened easily.

She pushed the window all the way open, resting her hands on the windowsill as she looked out over a view that harkened back to happier times in her life.

The ratcheting chirp of frogs laid down a tuneless song counterpointed by the velvet hoot of an owl.

She drew in a deep breath of the soft evening air, trying to imagine herself looking out over this whenever she wanted. It seemed like a dream that she hardly dared cling too hard to, for fear it would get taken away.

"Isn't it peaceful?" she said softly, her voice taking on a reverent tone. "I missed this place when we left."

"Why did you move away, Melanie?"

His quiet question eased past memories and emotions gently into the atmosphere.

"My father was always on the move." Melanie ran the palms of her hands over the blistered varnish of the windowsill. "He could never stay in one place longer than six months. He promised Derwin was going to be a last step. Though we did stay here the longest. Then another idea and a better opportunity came up and we were gone."

"I wondered what happened to you. One day you were at youth group and the next day you were gone."

In spite of the intervening years, Melanie's heart faltered. Memories and daydreams of Adam had taken up a large portion of that first year away. She had never considered that she had been other than a passing memory for him.

"Nice to know I was missed."

"You were."

"And you got to stay here," she said with a wistful sigh. "And end up in my dream home."

"It is a beautiful place."

Adam's brief agreement surprised her. Encouraged further disclosure. "When we moved away, I used to be homesick for this house. For the loving family that lived here."

"The Shewchuks?" Adam's voice held a disquieting note. It reminded her of other things he had said.

"When I first came here you mentioned something about not buying this house from a happy family," Melanie said, half turning to him. "What did you mean by that?"

His face was shadowed, his expression a mystery, save for the glint of his eyes, now a molten silver. "When we bought this house, Mrs. Shewchuk was a single mother, raising what was left of her family. This was about four years ago." He spoke softly, but Melanie could hear a trace of bitterness in his voice. "I'm sorry to bring a shadow to your memories, but this wasn't a happy family when she moved away."

The chill in the room grew with each word Adam spoke. Each word slowly dismembering the dreams she had clung to.

"How could that have happened?" Melanie murmured, shivering again. "Are you sure?"

"Of course I am. When we bought the house, Mr. Shewchuk had been gone for a number of years."

His casual words swept away the fragile dreams Melanie had spun around this house. It had always represented wholeness and completeness to her. She had clung to it when her own father left. When she and her mother were struggling along financially, just the two of them, she always thought of the Shewchuk family and this spacious home and lot. Thought of the fun times she'd had here. Thought of the faith of the family and the prayers she had learned here.

They, too, were now a broken family.

"That saddens me more than I can tell you" was all she said, turning back to the window. "I learned a lot of prayers here, downstairs at the table, and upstairs when I slept over. I thought they had such a strong faith in God."

"For what that's worth. God doesn't care about ordinary people. I can attest to that."

The bitterness that had been merely a trace was now a formidable force pushing against Melanie, his emotions completely at odds with the strong Christian youth she had admired.

Please, Lord, give me the right words. Help me show this hurting man that You still love him.

"He does care, Adam," Melanie said quietly, turning to him, drawn by the deep sorrow in his voice. "He also knows the pain of loss."

"But not of guilt."

That stopped her.

"What do you mean?"

He shifted his weight, dropped his shoulder against

the window frame beside her, his silver eyes watching her intently. "I've heard all my life about God's love. His justice. His punishment. But God is perfect. How can He understand the guilty burden of making a mistake?"

Disquiet nudged aside Melanie's calm assurances. "What mistakes are you talking about?"

Adam ran his hand over his hair and clutched the back of his neck as if holding back what Melanie sensed he wanted to tell her.

She remembered something Helen had said and carefully pressed on. "Are you talking about Lana?"

Adam closed his eyes. Dropped his head back against the wall. Drew in a deep breath.

"I never really wanted to live here," he murmured, massaging the back of his neck. "It was Lana's idea. Her dream. So was getting pregnant. It wasn't in the plan at all. The doctor warned her that there would be complications."

"Why?"

"Lana was a type-one diabetic. Insulin dependent. Pregnancy made her diabetes harder to control. Brittle, the doctor said. I wanted to move to the city, but Lana insisted we stay here."

He lowered his hand, slipped it into his pocket. Held her gaze, his own eyes steady, like a laser.

"When she started going into labor, she also started going into diabetic shock. The ambulance took too long to get here. Then she had to be airlifted to the city. Had we lived in the city, like I wanted, they could have saved her. Tiffany would have had a mother and I would have had a wife."

He spoke with a cold precision, as if each word was a scalpel cutting and slicing.

Melanie could picture the scene so vividly. The rocking ambulance, the intense efficiency of the paramedics as they tried desperately to keep life in this woman as her husband watched.

"I haven't been able to pray to that same God since," Adam said. "I don't believe He cares about ordinary people, so I don't think I need to waste His time."

She couldn't stop herself. She reached out to him and touched his arm, pressed her fingers against the smooth material of his worn shirt. She almost told him she was sorry, but those words couldn't wrap themselves around sorrow and deliver it back all clean and sanitized.

"God does care, Adam. He's always waiting for us to come to Him, to give Him our burdens." Her words fell into a silence that seemed to swallow them up.

"I sat and watched my wife die, Melanie." His anger pushed and pummeled her. "I prayed, I cried, but nothing. Nothing." He took a deep breath, turning his head away. "First He took my father, then my wife. I had to take a newborn baby home from the hospital because I didn't listen to my better judgment and God didn't listen to me."

Adam's arm stirred under her fingers, then he pushed himself away from the window. Away from her.

"Let's go look at the rest of the house."

He walked away, his footsteps echoing in the dark

quiet. But Melanie stayed behind, trying to collect her scattered thoughts. Impressions that had been turned around. Dumped out and rearranged.

His bitterness was so palpable, it seemed to linger in the room. Her only defense was prayer.

Please, Lord, let him feel Your love. Let him feel Your forgiveness.

Then she followed him down the hallway, going through the motions of looking at the other rooms, nodding sagely when he talked about glazed windows and the R-factor of the insulation. Inside, though, her mind was a swirling chaos of thoughts and impressions.

What dreams had Lana built around this house? What dreams had Adam lost with her death?

"These are the stairs to the attic, if you're interested." Adam had stopped in the center of the hallway, and was pulling on a rope.

Melanie wasn't really interested. Right now all she wanted was to go home and read her Bible. Find comfort in the only constant in her life.

But she had requested this tour. She knew she had to finish it.

A set of ladderlike stairs slipped down as silently as they ever had when Melanie had stayed here. "I think there's a few things here from the Shewchuk family that they didn't feel like taking with them. The renters moved them up here. You might find something there from your friend. I'll go on up first, make sure everything's okay." He easily clambered up the ladder.

Though Melanie's heart felt like a stone in her

chest, it was the mention of the Shewchuks that gave her the impetus to follow him up the stairs.

As she got to the top, Adam was waiting for her. She caught his extended hand, his fingers warm and strong around hers as he helped her the rest of the way up.

"Thanks," she said, curiously breathless, the air in the attic even more closed and stale than in the room they had just been in.

"No thanks needed," he said quietly, still holding her hand, his eyes on her.

Melanie gently pulled her hand back. Slowly looked away, far too aware of their situation. She felt secluded in the semidark of this closed-in space.

"There's a switch here somewhere," Adam murmured, taking a step away from her. Melanie didn't dare move, but as her eyes adjusted to the dark she could see humped shapes surrounding her. Boxes piled in one corner, and what looked to be a child's buggy. An old chest.

"Here it is."

The light exploded the darkness away and Melanie had to squint against the brightness.

"I was only up here a couple of times, checking out the insulation of the roof, so I'm not sure what's here." Adam walked away from Melanie, ducking his head as he walked along the length of the attic.

She looked around, the familiar objects bringing a flood of memories. An old quilt that had been thread-bare and moth-eaten when she and Dena had played here, now covered what looked to be a stack of old boxes. Beside that was a rusted-out electric fan, an old heater and an exercise bike with the chain broken off that she and Dena had pedaled on each day, trying to bring the odometer to a thousand kilometers.

What was in the boxes that no longer held any interest for Dena's family? Why hadn't they even bothered to come back for them?

"This looks interesting," Adam called out from the other end of the house, his voice muffled by the accumulated detritus of a family.

Melanie stepped around piled-up boxes and old furniture, her curiosity battling with a muted sorrow.

Adam pulled an old dresser away from behind another pile of boxes. It screeched a protest over the old dusty floor. "Looks like it's in pretty good shape yet."

"That was Mrs. Shewchuk's old dresser," Melanie murmured, running her hand over the familiar scarred wood. "I believe she got it from her mother." She stooped down, lifting the dainty metal handles now coated with rust. "I always thought it was such a beautiful piece of furniture, but it's really quite ordinary, isn't it?"

She tugged on one of the handles, but the drawer wouldn't move. The one above it was stuck, as well.

"Just needs a bit of gentle persuasion," Adam said, crouching down beside her. He gave a tug as well, but he wasn't successful, either.

His knee grazed her knee, his shoulder bumped against hers. She pulled herself abruptly to her feet, creating some distance.

"I guess its mysteries will stay mysteries," she

said with a light laugh, hoping to dispel her reaction to him.

"You can have it if you'd like." Still crouched down, Adam glanced up at her. "I certainly don't need it."

Melanie touched the dresser again, as if making a connection between the harsh present and the gentle memories of the past. Her memories were valid, and no one could take them away.

"It's just going to sit up here and molder unless you want to wait until you take possession of the house."

"I'd love to put it back in their bedroom," Melanie said, her finger tracing a scratch on the surface. "I remember sneaking in there with Dena to look at the old picture albums she had in the bottom drawer."

"Maybe they're still there," Adam said, giving the drawer another tug.

"I'm pretty sure she would take them along with her," Melanie said. She brushed her hands over her hips. "But if you're serious about the offer, I'd love to have the dresser. It's no antique, but it does bring back some fond memories."

"I can move it downstairs for you and take a better look at it. Get the drawers working."

"Do you need some help?"

Adam glanced pointedly at her dress and Melanie followed his gaze. "Guess not," she said ruefully.

"I'll do it some other time." He clambered down the stairs and waited for her at the bottom of the ladder as he had previously at the top. Again he took her hand, helping her down the last awkward steps, reminding Melanie of servants helping elegantly dressed ladies of another era descend from horse-drawn coaches.

It made her feel curiously protected.

And more aware of Adam than she liked. His harsh comment about God still weighed on her mind. It created a distance she needed to maintain.

In spite of her yearning for a family, and her own youthful crush on Adam, she knew that he was not the one to help her dream come true. Not as long as he stayed estranged from God.

"I'd better be leaving," she said as they reached the kitchen. She slipped her purse over her shoulder and angled him a casual smile. "I'll see you on Monday."

But just as she turned, she caught his glance and a glimpse of a deep longing, so brief she thought she'd imagined it.

Chapter Five

"So when do you leave with the little munchkin for Disneyland?" Kyle asked. It was Monday, and the day had not started well.

Adam tucked the phone under his ear, his hands clumsily braiding Tiffany's hair. He wanted to say more to his partner, but his mother sat two feet away from him, so he replied with an ambiguous "A couple of days." He had only a few days to get his mother moved before he left. And he was having no success with that, either.

"I guess there's no way I can talk you out of that?"

"The tickets are bought, Kyle. All the plans are in place." He wasn't going to tell Kyle that he might have to cancel his trip if he didn't find a way to get his mother moved. Whether Kyle liked it or not, Adam needed some time away from him and his relentless demands, phone calls and pressure.

"The reason I ask is that I'm swamped here," Kyle

continued, his voice rising. "The bid we put in on the Sarcee mall has been accepted. Conditionally."

"What condition?" He and Kyle had sweated over that bid, sat up until two, three in the morning running the figures through the calculator until he knew them by rote. What was there left that the company wanted?

Just at that moment Tiffany pulled her head away. Adam lost his grip on the phone and it tumbled to the floor.

He bit back an angry retort, let go of Tiffany's hair and picked up the phone. "You still there, Kyle?"

"Yeah. The condition is our liability insurance. What about the house? Is the money going to come through on that?"

"Nothing definite has been signed. I just said I had someone interested."

"Well, we could use the money from that really bad. Give me a call tonight and let me know if you can put off that trip to Disneyland with your girl. I really, really need you here, man. Did you get that bid done on the Anderson home?"

"Still working on it." Adam grimaced at the piles of paper perched on one corner of the kitchen table. He and Kyle didn't need the job, but Kyle liked to cover all angles—put bids in on any potential job.

Trouble was, if this mall deal fell through, they might need the job. Kyle hated missing the tiniest opportunity to turn over a dollar. "Let me know when you can come back to Calgary."

Adam stifled a retort and tried to push down his growing anger with Kyle. He hadn't even agreed to

Kyle's request, and resented the implication that all Kyle had to do was ask and Adam would come running. "I'll see what I can do," he said, keeping his reply deliberately ambiguous.

Adam hung up the phone and turned back to his daughter. Tiffany was running her hands over her head, disheveling the braid he had half done.

"Tiffany, sweetie, don't." He reached for the brush, but she twisted her head away from him.

"Do you want me to do that?" Helen asked, looking up from the book she was reading.

"I think I should be able to manage." Adam followed Tiffany's head with the brush, but succeeded only in getting it tangled in her curls.

By the time he got the brush out of her hair she was crying, her hands working at her eyes spreading her tears all over her face.

Since she'd got up this morning, she had been alternately contrary and cranky, not listening to anything he said. He wondered what she was going to be like at Disneyland. Wondered if he should do as his partner suggested and just forget the whole thing and go back to Calgary.

He picked up the hairbrush.

"Why don't you wait until Melanie comes?" Helen suggested. "She could do Tiffany's hair."

"I'm sure she doesn't have time for that."

"I'm sure she would. Melanie is such a caring person."

Adam made a noncommittal noise vague enough to show he was listening, yet relaying nothing his mother could build on. But he put the brush down and pulled out the container of cocoa for Tiffany's chocolate milk.

The morning had not gone well. He had spent the past hour on the phone trying to organize an ambulance and a home-care worker in Calgary for his mother. None of his phone calls had been very successful. Time was running out, and now Kyle was pressuring him to come back.

"The barbecue Melanie was talking about was on the bulletin. Are you going to go?"

Adam gave the milk another stir, clanking the spoon loudly against the side of the glass, trying to think of a suitable response for his mother. If he could get his ducks in a row, he and his mother wouldn't be here in Derwin on the weekend.

"I asked Melanie if I could go. She said it wasn't a good idea," his mother continued with a light sigh, in spite of Adam's silence. "I remember you talking about her when you were in high school. Didn't you used to like her?"

"I was eighteen and she was all of fourteen, Mother."

Adam would have had to be deaf not to hear the hopeful tone in his mother's voice and blind not to see where his mother was leading. Only, he wasn't following.

Adam didn't deny Melanie's good looks, or her kindness or how considerate she was. Or that he used to think she was cute and spunky. Right now he didn't have the space for a woman. Especially not a woman who spoke so easily of a God he used to believe in but couldn't get close to anymore.

"Here's your chocolate, Tiff." He set the glass in front of his daughter.

"Don't want it," she said with a dark pout, pushing at the glass. Milk spilled all over the table, narrowly missing the papers he was working on.

Impatience burst through him. He closed his eyes and counted slowly to ten. Then he rescued the Anderson quote and the house estimate for Melanie from the spreading brown puddle.

"You said you wanted chocolate milk, Tiff," he said sternly as he swiped at the chocolate mess with a damp cloth.

He rinsed the cloth out and finished the job. Tiffany was now running her sticky hands through her hair, further disheveling it. "Tiffany, don't do that."

"Go to Gramma."

"Wait. I'm going to do your hair again." It would be easier if he got her hair cut, but her long curls were the only part of her that reminded him of Lana. He didn't have the heart.

"I don't think she's going to sit still long enough for you to do a proper job," Helen said.

Tiffany started crying, pushing Adam's hands away as he tried to redo her braids.

He didn't need this, he thought, picking up the elastics Tiffany had thrown on the floor. Maybe Kyle was right. Maybe he should cancel his trip and get his mother settled into the fifty-plus condo he had picked out for her. He could put his daughter back into the day care and he could go back to work where skill saws whined, air hammers pounded, compressors rattled.

It almost seemed peaceful compared to heading off to Disneyland with a daughter who didn't want to have anything to do with him.

"Hello, everyone." Melanie's voice sounded at the back door and Adam stifled a groan.

Of course Melanie would have to come in the middle of the chaos.

"How are you, Helen?" she asked, setting her bag on the floor beside his mother's chair.

Adam, all too aware of his mother's previous comments, merely gave Melanie a quick nod and turned his attention back to his daughter's mop of curls.

She squirmed away from him. When she saw Melanie she pushed her hands against the table. "Want to go down. Now."

"Just wait, Tiffany. I need to do your hair."

Tiffany started to cry again, twisting her head this way and that. "No. Don't want you. Want her."

Tiffany's words plunged like a knife into his heart. He stared down at her, his hands now hanging idle by his sides as the words his tiny girl had thrown at him reverberated in the sudden silence.

"Tiffany, come to Gramma," Helen said quietly. "Adam, we can watch her while you move that dresser."

As Tiffany clambered out of the chair, Adam looked up in time to see Melanie's gaze on his. He almost cringed at the sympathy he saw there.

He tossed the elastics on the table and left. As his mother said, he had a dresser to move.

Melanie watched Adam go, wishing she dared say something. But though her heart ached for him, she doubted he would appreciate or welcome any advice she could give him.

"Please forgive my son," Helen said quietly, stroking Tiffany's hair. "He's not been having a good morning. He's leaving for Disneyland soon and he can't seem to get an ambulance organized to move me to the city."

"That is too bad," Melanie agreed halfheartedly. Obviously Adam was still going through with his plans. The thought bothered her more than it should have.

"He says he's found one of those fifty-plus places for me to go." Helen twisted one of Tiffany's curls around her finger. "Said I would enjoy it. What do you think?"

Melanie felt torn. She had promised Adam she would help him get his mother ready to move. Yet she fully understood where Helen was coming from. The more excited Melanie got about owning her first home, the more she understood Helen's reluctance to leave. Leave this house. Leave Derwin and the community she was a part of.

She knew how much her mother would have loved to live here.

"I think that for now we need to concentrate on getting you back in shape as much as possible," she said, sidestepping the question and her own opinions.

Half an hour later Helen was sitting back in her chair, slightly flushed from the exercises Melanie had her doing.

"So how am I doing?" Helen asked as Melanie packed up her nurse's kit.

"Truthfully, I was hoping you'd be a little further along by now." Melanie rolled up the blood pressure cuff and placed it in her bag. "How have you been feeling otherwise?"

Helen sighed. "I want to feel better, but I feel so weak all the time. And I get so many headaches."

"It will take a while for your new medication to help," Melanie said, though she doubted the new medication would fix what was really wrong with Helen. Her problems were emotional rather than physical and the only thing that would cure that wasn't going to happen. "Now, let's get you back to your bedroom." Melanie turned back to Tiffany. "Are you going to come to Gramma's room? Or should we find your dad?"

"Go to Gramma's room." Tiffany yanked Melanie's stethoscope off her neck. Melanie rescued it just before she dropped it on the floor. Tiffany scrambled to her feet and ran over to her grandma's side. "I help you."

Helen wasn't quite as flushed by the time Melanie had her settled in. Tiffany was once again busy with the crayons and coloring books that lay on a small desk that was new to the room.

"You're okay with Tiffany in here?" Melanie asked.

Helen just nodded and smiled down at her granddaughter. "I may as well enjoy her company while I can," she said with a pensive look.

"You rest now."

Melanie crouched down and fingered a curl away

from Tiffany's face. She had finished the braiding job that Adam had started, but the little girl's hair had a curl that escaped even the tightest braid. "You be good now for your gramma, okay?"

Tiffany smiled up at her, her angelic expression a direct contrast to the scowl that had twisted her face when Melanie had first arrived.

Melanie stroked her soft cheek, a swift uplifting rush of affection spiraling through her. "That's a good girl," she said softly. "I'll go find Adam and tell him where you are." She closed the door behind her. The short hallway gave way to the kitchen. Sunshine bathed the room, warm and welcoming. Melanie's heart thrilled with a sense of ownership. In a few weeks, Lord willing, this was going to be hers. It seemed too wonderful for her mind to accept.

Please Lord, let it happen.

Adam bit his lip as he stared down at the steep stairs. It was going to be trickier getting the dresser down than he had calculated. Gravity and the angle of the stairs were his nemesis.

He worked the dresser as close to the stairs as he dared and laid it on its back, letting it slide over the opening. He grabbed the rope he had tied around it, braced his feet against the top rung of the ladder and eased the dresser down the stairs, slowing its descent with the rope.

The stairs creaked and the rope jerked hard. Then as he watched in disbelief, the stairs gave way, the dresser heaved the rope out of his hands and crashed to the floor below.

Wood splintered. The dresser split and settled.

He closed his eyes, his heart beating against his ribs.

"Adam, are you all right?" Melanie called out from the bottom of the stairs.

"I'm okay," he replied, surveying with dismay the wreckage below him. Why not this on top of everything else?

Melanie was already running up the stairs. She swung around the newel post at the top and skidded to a halt when she saw the twisted wood of what was left of the dresser Adam knew she had prized.

He felt sick.

He dropped down from the attic, using what was left of the ladder.

"Are you sure you're okay?" Melanie asked, looking up at him.

"I'm fine," he said with disgust. "I wish I could say the same about the dresser."

"What happened?"

"Near as I can tell, the stairs gave way." A cold finger of dread shivered down his spine as he spoke. This could just as easily have happened when Melanie was climbing up the stairs the other night.

Melanie crouched beside the dresser, touching it lightly. "Well, I guess we'll get to find out what was in that bottom drawer," she said with a light laugh, tugging at a lower panel that was now awry.

How could she joke about this?

"You're going to get splinters." Once again Adam knelt beside her, taking her hands away from the dresser. "I'm really sorry about this. I feel terrible."

Melanie jerked her hands back, creating a moment of added awkwardness. "Don't feel bad. Please. It was a gift. I didn't know anything about this a week ago." She put her hands on her knees to get up. Stopped.

"What's this?" In spite of Adam's warning, she tugged on a drawer front that had split away. With a creak of loose nails it separated from the sides of the drawer, exposing a cardboard box. Melanie pulled it out and opened it.

"It's full of envelopes," she said, sitting back on her knees as she flipped through the contents with her index finger. "All addressed to Donna Shewchuk. They all come from the same person. Jason Shewchuk. Donna's husband."

"I thought he had left her." Adam frowned, turning the envelope over. "It's not opened."

Melanie took it back, looked it over herself. Then checked out the letters in the box. "There must be about twenty letters in here. And only two of them have been opened."

Adam held out his hand for the box and checked for himself. "He's traveled a few places," he murmured, glancing over the return addresses. "I wonder if they got delivered."

"They're all in this box. Someone gathered them together."

"What are the dates of the cancellation?"

Melanie read a few out. "From what I can see they are about six years old."

Adam tapped the envelope on his hand, thinking.

"She had the house rented out for a couple of years while she was trying to sell it. I wonder if they were coming here then and the renters didn't bother to pass them on."

"What are you going to do about them?"

"I'm not sure." He put the letters back in the box and closed the lid.

"It would be nice if we could get them to Mrs. Shewchuk somehow," Melanie said.

"She might not like what's in them."

Melanie didn't reply, but Adam could tell from the wistful look on her face that she didn't believe him. He wished he could understand her eternal optimism.

"Is Tiffany with my mother?" he asked, pushing himself up.

"She's coloring. I think she'll be okay for a little while. She seems quite content around your mother." Melanie got to her feet, brushing the front of her pants. "I was just leaving, so if there's anything else…" She let the sentence drag.

Adam hesitated, looked down at the box of letters, then up at Melanie. "Do you have a bit of time yet?"

"Sure."

He walked with her down the stairs, his steps slow and measured as Melanie sorted through her emotions and reactions to this man.

She shouldn't have come on Saturday night for supper. It had shifted their relationship and called up older emotions and feelings that had no place in the present. And just now, as they'd been sorting through the letters, she'd felt a curious connection and a curious newer attraction.

The screen door slapped shut behind them. Melanie walked over to the railing of the porch. Ignoring the paint flecking off it, she leaned back against the sun-warmed wood, curiosity warring with a new tenderness.

"I'm almost done with the quote on the house," Adam said, his hands settled on his hips. "I'll get it finished by tomorrow. Hopefully."

She wasn't going to ask him how it looked. She had made up her mind that one way or another she was going to have this house. Each visit confirmed her desire, cemented it. In spite of the house's history, it was still the home she wanted.

"I'm also really sorry about the dresser."

"We covered this already," Melanie said, setting her nurse's bag on the porch floor.

"I know how much it would have meant to you to have something from the Shewchuks. I'd like to try to fix it up, though I'm not sure I'll be very successful." Adam shoved one hand through his hair, then looked back at Melanie, his expression intent. "Actually I didn't really want to just talk about the dresser. The main reason I asked you to stay is about my daughter. Tiffany."

Melanie saw once again a shadow of the pain she'd seen in his face before. She thought of the little run-in she'd witnessed this morning.

"I don't know what to do about her. She won't listen to me and, as I said before, she seems to connect with anyone else but me."

"Have you noticed this before?"

Adam was quiet. He chewed his lower lip, looking beyond her. "What I have noticed is she has never spontaneously come to me. Never looked me straight in the eye." He drew in a slow breath, looking beyond Melanie. "She has never called me 'Daddy.'"

The raw pain in his voice twisted her heart, called to a lonely part of her own life. A part that yearned for a man to call "Daddy." Yearned for a man who had been a sporadic part of her life until he died.

"How long would you work each day?" she asked, keeping her voice soft, nonjudgmental.

Adam frowned and tugged at his lower lip. "I had to pull my share of the load. My partner has been in the business for a few years." He looked up at her, his eyes bleak with remembered sorrow. "I had to work fourteen-hour days to catch up. I needed to make sure I could give Tiffany whatever she needed."

And you had a wife's death that you were trying to forget. A guilt you were trying to outrun, Melanie thought.

"It's that kind of business, Melanie," he continued, his arms folded over his chest. "This is seasonal work, and you've got to work when you can. You can't afford to miss out on any opportunities. There's too many other businesses ready to jump in."

"Yet you made the decision to get away in the middle of the summer to take your daughter to Disneyland," Melanie coaxed gently, ignoring his defensive posture.

Adam gave her a crooked smile that lacked any

humor or warmth. "The day-care supervisor suggested that I spend some time with her. Said that Tiffany was developing attachment problems. Whatever that means."

Melanie sent up a small prayer of gratitude to the underappreciated people who took care of other people's children and cared enough to get involved.

"Tiffany has had her routine in the city and she has been comfortable with that. And, though it's hard to say, it doesn't sound like you were a part of it. Now—" Melanie lifted her hands in a helpless gesture "—she's around you all the time and she's not used to it."

"So I should probably take her back to her normal routine, is what you're saying, instead of going to Disneyland."

Melanie shook her head, sorrow flitting through her. "Disneyland is not the answer to your problem, nor is it going to be a problem. You could go, but nothing will change if you do. You could go back to Calgary and the same thing will happen. I'm saying that this little girl doesn't know where she fits in your life."

She knew the words would hurt, but hadn't been able to think of a softer way to deliver them.

"But I thought being around her all the time would help."

"Not at a place like Disneyland."

"But I only have so much time."

You have all the time you need, she thought. If you set your priorities right.

But she couldn't tell him that.

"You wanted to talk about Tiffany. You obviously know that things aren't the way they should be." Melanie pushed herself away from the porch railing, unable to keep her distance. "You care about your daughter. Anyone can see that. But now you need to figure out how you are going to be the father that she so badly needs."

"And what about a mother? Doesn't she need that, too?" The pain was there again in his eyes, and jealousy feathered Melanie's heart at his bleak words.

"She has you, Adam," Melanie said softly, touching him lightly on the arm. "And you're the parent she needs right now."

"So what do I do? She is all I have."

Melanie looked up at Adam and felt a rush of warmth for this man who was so obviously concerned, yet confused.

Adam might not be doing everything right, but she sensed that he was trying. She doubted her father had ever expended the same amount of energy on her needs. Her wishes.

Please, Lord. Help me say the right thing. Help me show him what he really needs.

"I think you need to give her a little bit of space. Let her figure out how she's going to fit in your life." Melanie bit her lip, hesitated, then plunged on. "The only way this is going to work is over a period of time. You said you had your vacation booked—spend those days here. With your daughter. Be with her, but not so intensely involved in everything she does. And at the same time, when she does respond to you, be available for her. Don't call your partner every day.

Don't get distracted by your work. Don't do up quotes and make phone calls. Don't let other outside things intrude on this time. And don't take her to Disneyland. It's just noise and entertainment for a girl too young to appreciate it. You won't make a connection with so many distractions around.''

Adam ran his hand over his face, then glanced at Melanie. "What do I do with the tickets?"

"I'm sure you could sell them."

"You realize that will mean staying here for the next two weeks. I thought you would want me gone so you could buy the house?"

"I do. As we speak I am arranging financing and transferring money, but you know I won't be taking possession right away. And your relationship with your daughter is more important than this house."

"So why are you trying to get me to stay here as long as possible?" He quirked a crooked smile and Melanie felt an indefinable tension loosen as other emotions gripped her heart at his question.

"Maybe I'm hoping you'll decide to put some of your talents to work and fix up a few things during that time?" Melanie injected a teasing note in her voice to offset her reaction.

"It's actually close to three weeks, but I wasn't going to tell my mother that." He pulled his lower lip between his teeth and looked out over the yard, his hands resting on his hips. "You really think this is going to make a difference?"

Beneath his casual tone Melanie heard the pain in his voice. "It's a start. And a good one." She couldn't help but touch him again, wanting to reassure him. "You care about your daughter and that gives you a lot."

Adam drew in a deep breath, half turning to her. "Thanks, Melanie. I appreciate your honesty. And your advice." He covered her hand with his. She could feel the calluses, the rough skin. The hands of a working man.

His clear blue eyes held hers and Melanie's mind easily sifted back, remembering a young man coming to her rescue. A man who was now in need of rescue himself.

"I'll be praying for you," she couldn't help but say, drawn to the man he was, the man who now stood in front of her.

Adam blinked, dropped his hand. "For what that's worth," he said, slipping his hands into his pockets.

His words were like a shot of cold water. And in a way she was thankful he had spoken them.

She knew her feelings for him were changing, moving toward dangerous ground. And now she was going to be seeing him every day for the next few weeks.

She hoped she could remember this and other conversations.

She knew it was going to be difficult.

Chapter Six

"So how has it been, working with the infamous Adam Engler?"

Melanie looked up from the form she was filling out to see Serena Davis, a fellow worker, standing by her desk. The expectant look on Serena's face belied the sophisticated air she carried as easily as the tailored suits she favored.

Serena had been an answer to a prayer for Melanie. When she first moved to Derwin it was Serena who had helped her find an apartment, had shown up that first evening at the apartment with a casserole and some friends.

"And what is he supposedly infamous for?" Melanie sat back in her swivel chair, balancing her pen between her fingers.

Serena smoothed a hand over her dark hair, though not a strand of it was out of place, and leaned her hip against the desk as if settling in for a long gossipy chat. "Local boy loses wife. Takes baby daughter and moves his handsome self off to Calgary, cowboy-hat capital of Canada.'' Serena used her perfectly manicured index finger to tick off Adam's offenses. ''Starts construction company. Cuts off all communication with family. Mortal sins in a town like Derwin, where everyone always knows what everyone else is doing. And especially troublesome when said local boy is as good-looking as Adam Engler is.''

''I'm sure Adam had his reasons,'' Melanie said, preferring to err on the side of caution rather than speculate aloud.

Serena laughed. ''Bless you for being so discreet, Melanie. I was trying to be facetious. Obviously a bit heavy-handed.'' Serena fingered the gold chain around her neck. ''The other day I was chatting with Sandy Gerrard, Lana's sister. She used to always be checking on Lana. Like a little mother hen. She happened to mention that they haven't seen Adam or Tiffany yet. Did he refer to them at all?''

Melanie blew out a sigh. She should have known this was going to come up sooner or later. In a small town, people not only knew each other's business, they made it a point that other people fill in the gaps in their own information database.

''I guess you'll have to talk to Adam on that,'' she said with a quick smile.

''Oh, don't get all professional and haul out client confidentiality. That doesn't work in Derwin.'' Serena tapped her lower lip with her thumb, her eyes on Melanie. ''I guess I was hoping you might mention the family to him. Maybe let him know that they'd really like to see Tiffany and him sometime.''

"I thought Helen was my patient?" Melanie stifled her annoyance. First Adam wanted her help to get his mother to move, now Serena wanted her to help Adam reconcile with his in-laws. She should have asked for a more clear-cut job description.

"We deal with the whole patient here," Serena tut-tutted, a twinkle in her eye. "And if that means peripheral family relations, then that must be dealt with as well."

"I think that's just an official way to be nosy."

"Informed," Serena corrected. She pushed away from the desk. "Are you coming to the community barbecue this weekend?"

"I don't know. Been thinking about it."

Serena dismissed Melanie's wavering with a flash of her carnation-colored nails. "Do more than think. The new superintendent who is currently reviewing your application for the full-time position you applied for will be coming." Serena pointed at Melanie. "Though you'll probably get the job anyhow, it wouldn't hurt to meet her face-to-face and let her know what an asset you'll be to this health unit."

"Thanks for the tip."

"You'll need the job if you're going to buy that house."

"How did you know about the house?" Melanie dropped her pen on the desk with a clatter that mirrored her faint annoyance. "I haven't even signed the offer to purchase yet."

"We don't have the party-line telephone anymore, but we still have information exchange." Serena gave her a patronizing look. "Coffee shop? Floyd talking to another couple interested in the house? Serena overhearing your name being mentioned?'' She lifted her hands in a ''what could I do'' gesture.

Melanie's heart tripped at the thought of someone else wanting the house. The last time she had spoken to Floyd she was the only one who had put in an offer, but it frightened her to think that someone else was interested. ''Thanks for the tip on the barbecue. I'll be there.''

''I have my ulterior motives. I'm hoping you might need me to visit Helen sometime.'' Serena winked as she pushed herself away from Melanie's desk. ''Wouldn't mind making Adam's acquaintance again. If you get my meaning.''

As Serena walked away, Melanie recalled Roxanne's exuberant greeting to Adam.

Adam created a flutter in many a woman's heart, her own included.

She remembered the touch of his hand on hers. The way his eyes crinkled when he smiled, which wasn't often, and felt her own heart respond.

But superimposed over her reaction were his bitter remarks.

''He's not for you,'' she whispered, bending over the forms she was filling out. The fact that she was buying his house should serve as enough of a reminder. He was leaving. She was staying.

''Are you sure you don't need a ride home?'' Bob Tessier lingered in the foyer of the church as Melanie slipped her sweater on.

"Thanks, Bob. I only live a few blocks away. I prefer to walk."

And I prefer not to give you any ideas.

She tempered her thoughts with a smile as she lifted her hair free from the back of her sweater. "It gives me a chance to practice some of the new parts our choir director gave us."

Bob's smile sagged ever so slightly. "Then I'll be seeing you at the bank whenever you get the information from Adam."

"He said he was going to be bringing the estimate over tonight, so I'll be in some time this week." She pulled her sweater closer around her, gave Bob another polite smile. "Well, I better go. Thanks again for the offer." And before he could forestall her with anything else, Melanie left.

When she came around the building, as was her usual habit, she veered away from the sidewalk leading to the street and toward the tree line separating the cemetery from the church parking lot. The summer evening held a light chill with a hint of rain in the air.

When Trudy Visser's will was read, Melanie had been surprised to discover that she had wanted to be buried in Derwin. It seemed her mother had shared her attachment to the small town.

So now, each time Melanie was at the church, she took the time to visit her mother's grave. It had become a small connection to a parent who had given Melanie everything she could. And it was a way of cementing Melanie's desire to put down roots in this town.

She wasn't alone this time, however.

A single pickup was parked by the trees bordering the graveyard. As she came closer, she recognized the truck.

And facing his wife's gravestone stood Adam, his cap in his hand.

He bent down on one knee, his finger tracing Lana's name. Then he lowered his head into his hands, closing his eyes.

Was he praying? Berating God? Missing his wife?

Helen frequently fretted that Adam didn't seem to have any interest in women. It had been three years since Lana had died—surely it was time he try to find someone again, she had said, giving Melanie a look rife with innuendo. But Melanie had wisely let the comment slide.

Now, as Melanie watched, Adam got slowly to his feet, his hands working the bill of his cap. His features were twisted in sorrow.

Adam slipped his cap back on his head and Melanie turned away, afraid to be discovered watching him. She walked to her mother's gravestone as a faint jealousy for Adam's devotion to his wife fought with her own sorrow.

She stopped in front of the granite slab and, as always, was unable to connect the memories of her mother with the cold precision of Trudy Visser's name cut into the stone. Though she had witnessed the body being lowered into the grave and had made most of the preparations herself, she still couldn't accept that her mother was no more. She would no longer call her at work. No longer be standing at the stove, cooking up yet another pot of soup, when Melanie would stop by her apartment.

Just as Adam had, she bent and touched her mother's name, surprised at how cold the stone felt under her fingers.

Someday, Lord, I'll see her again. Until then, help me to carry on.

She swallowed a knot of pain as she lifted her face to the sky overhead, as if hoping to catch even a faint glimpse of her mother in glory.

But all she saw was a hawk wheeling on an updraft against a faint wisp of a cloud.

"Hey, Melanie."

Adam spoke quietly, but she still jumped.

"Sorry," he said with a gentle smile. "I didn't mean to startle you. I saw you here, so figured I'd come over and say hi." He looked past her at the stone at her feet. "She died only a year ago?"

Melanie nodded, slowly gaining equilibrium. "She wanted to be buried in Derwin when she died. I guess we both liked it here enough to stay. One way or the other."

"Do you miss her?"

His question caught her off balance. Other than Helen, no one had even mentioned her mother. Though she realized they hadn't been here long enough those many years ago to make a lot of connections, it still hurt.

"Yes. I do," she answered softly, blinking back an unexpected moisture at his consideration. "She was my mother, but she was also my good friend."

Then Melanie felt his hand on her shoulder. Just a

light touch, barely discernible through the material of her sweater, but the connection felt better than she wanted to admit.

Since her mother's death she had been all alone, and it wasn't a situation she relished. Nor did she know how to change it. She had no father and no siblings. The various men she had dated all wanted to make their home in the city, and she hadn't found anyone for whom she was willing to sacrifice her dream of living in Derwin.

"It's hard to let go," Melanie said quietly. "I have to confess, I saw you at Lana's grave. I imagine you know only too well how I feel."

Adam lowered his hand, as if mention of his wife created a barrier between them. "That was three years ago," he said brusquely.

Then silence.

Melanie wanted to breach the gap, but was afraid of saying the wrong thing. So she settled for the practical.

"How is the estimate coming?"

"I have it in the truck," Adam said. "I was going to bring them over, but you weren't home."

"Choir practice." Melanie hugged herself again. She risked a quick glance at Adam, disconcerted to find his steady gaze on her. And equally disconcerted to find herself unable to look away.

Adam broke the connection first, taking a step back. Looking away. "I'll get the papers for you." He strode away, and Melanie realized with a sinking feeling that she had done that all wrong, as well. She should have invited him to her apartment. They could have visited over a cup of coffee.

And talked about what? Dead relatives?

Adam came back quite quickly, file folder in hand. He flipped it open, looking down at the contents. "It's all itemized. I would have printed it out, but I don't have access to a computer." He closed it again and handed it to her with a rueful smile. "I tried to be honest and fair. I hope this is what you need."

Melanie forced a smile to her face. "Thanks. I'll look it over tonight."

Adam slipped his hands into his back pockets, rocking back on his heels.

Ask him now.

But he glanced at his watch, the eternal gesture denoting it was time to go.

"If I have any questions I'll call you," she said, beating him to it. "Thanks again." She didn't want to hang around extending the awkwardness of the moment. Like some overeager teenage girl waiting to be asked to the prom.

As she walked away she sighed. She hadn't handled that well at all.

Guess it was another evening in front of the television.

The file folder felt heavy in her hands, and her apartment seemed even quieter than usual when she let herself in. She slipped her coat off, hung it up and dropped into the nearest chair with the estimate.

She paged through it, her heart growing heavier with each line.

And when she read the final figure, she dropped

her head back against the chair and blew out a sigh. The number was larger than she had thought it would be.

She had some big decisions to make.

"This one is a lovely two-bedroom bungalow that I know is in your price range and won't need any work. Basically turnkey." Floyd stopped his vehicle in front of a white picket fence. "I think you might like this one."

Melanie obediently looked at the house beyond the bright yellow for-sale sign tacked to the fence.

She tried to work up some enthusiasm for the tidy white house perched on a lawn so green she felt like Dorothy in the Emerald City. Tiger lilies grew in mass profusion in one corner of the lawn and plump cedar bushes softened the front entrance. It was lovely. And, as Floyd had said, well within her price range. It was only two blocks from the park. Three blocks from the bank. Five blocks from the grocery store and only seven blocks away from the auction market.

Location, location, location.

"It's lovely."

"Now, why do I sense a great big *but* in your voice?" Floyd said with a laugh.

Because it's not the house with the turret. It's not the house that I've been dreaming about since I moved away from here. The house that needs so much work that if I buy it, I'll be in debt for thirty years.

After reading Adam's estimate and doing a little book work of her own, Melanie had realized that if she bought the house she would be stretching herself beyond comfortable boundaries. So she had phoned Floyd, just to give herself a few other options.

"I do have another place out in Eastbar, but I know you wanted to live in Derwin," Floyd continued. "And there's a larger house on the outskirts of town that is more expensive, but it's brand-new."

"Let's have a look at the new house," Melanie said, turning away from the charming home that just didn't create any zing for her. She wanted to be fair and do justice to this comparison shopping she was indulging in.

The other house was also lovely. Because it was new, the landscaping was minimal. A few scraggly trees were parked on the corners of the lot, held up by guy wires. In a few years they would be fuller and taller.

The first thing she saw was a large two-car garage, its double door like a wide yawning mouth that had gobbled up the rest of the house. The living room, though substantial, looked tiny tucked alongside the garage.

Melanie looked around at the rest of the houses, each as large as the one in front of her, each boasting the same dominant garage. It didn't look like a neighborhood—it looked like a parking garage.

"Did you want to see the inside of the house?"

Melanie sighed. She felt she had to give this place a chance, but she knew it would be a waste of time. The neighborhood looked stark, unwelcoming. At least the little white house looked as if it belonged to a community. It had history and probably its own stories, happy and sad.

And if she bought that house, her payments wouldn't be as steep.

"Let's go look at the little white house again. I'd like to see the inside."

Floyd just smiled.

She got her tour, and she found that the house was even more charming on the inside than the outside. It would be a perfect home for her, she thought, standing in the kitchen, looking out over a large backyard. Not too large. Convenient.

But it didn't give her the same sense of belonging that she felt in the Shewchuk house. Correction, the Engler house.

Was she pinning too much on dreams and wishes that, if Adam were right, were just illusions and fantasies?

"I'll need some time to think about it," she said, turning back to Floyd.

"You've got my number." He smiled at her and escorted her back out of the house.

"By the way," she said as he drove her back home, "you said there was another couple interested in the Engler house. How serious are they?"

Floyd pursed his lips and waggled his hand back and forth. "I think they're like you. They see the work it needs and are having second thoughts. I've shown them the houses I showed you this evening, as well. I'm pretty sure they're going to put in an offer on the house in the new subdivision."

Relief plunged through her, leaving her almost

breathless. "So there's no one else interested in it, then?"

"Now that you've backed out, no. No one."

Melanie worried her lower lip with her teeth, thinking. Planning. She was crazy to think about buying the Engler house. Her practical nature told her that.

So why couldn't she get it off her mind? Why did these other perfectly suitable and charming homes not give her the same sense of home that run-down house did?

Floyd stopped in front of her apartment and turned to her. "You're going to go for the Engler house, aren't you?"

"What makes you say that?"

"Eighteen years in the business, that's what."

Melanie sighed, toying with the strap of her purse. "I keep coming back to it. I know it's crazy and maybe not the best investment I could make, but I really, really want that house. These other homes were nice, but they just don't…" She hesitated, not wanting to sound like a complete lunatic. "I don't know, they just don't call to me."

"I'd pay attention to that," Floyd said with a grin. "And if that's the case…" Floyd opened his briefcase and pulled out a few papers. "This is an offer to purchase. I'm not pressuring you, but if you're serious about buying the house, we need to fill one of these out."

Melanie slipped the papers into her purse and walked slowly to her apartment building. This was going to take some more thought. And some more prayer.

Chapter Seven

$\sim\!\!\sim$

They fit. Adam felt a gentle rush of accomplishment when the dovetail joints of the drawer slid perfectly into each other. Not even a gap, he mused, running his finger over the joint. Tomorrow he could put the fronts on the drawers, and once the glue was dry he could assemble it.

Knowing he still had the touch gave him more of a thrill than he would have realized.

And his daughter crouched at his feet, happily playing in the wood shavings, created a lingering satisfaction that superseded the fit of the dresser drawer.

The original chest of drawers that Melanie had desired had been shattered beyond repair. While rummaging through his tools and the pieces of lumber he had lying around, hoping to fix it, he had decided to build her a replica. A reminder of good memories. And it would serve the dual purpose of keeping him busy in a place his daughter could be, as well.

But a curious thing had happened as he worked

with the wood. He'd found a satisfaction seeping through his day that he hadn't felt in a long time.

He and his partner specialized in large buildings. Structures of concrete and steel that captured air and space with harsh angles, put together by large pieces of equipment.

But this work he could see take shape under his own hands. As the frame was put together, the drawers took shape, a dormant serenity began to surface. He realized how much he missed working directly with a project, touching it and feeling it take shape as he had when he worked with Lana's father.

"Bess a litto am tonight. Bess a litto am tonight." Tiffany crouched in the shavings at his feet singing the same line over and over. His mother had taught her the song and Tiffany remembered only part of it. What she lacked in repertoire she more than made up for in enthusiasm.

She threw a handful of shavings up in the air, laughing as they twisted down, liberally coating her hair and clinging to her coveralls. Her face was still sticky from the Popsicle his mother had given her, her one braid had come loose again, but she had a look of peace on her face he hadn't seen in a while.

The first morning he'd started working on the dresser, she had stayed with him only a few minutes and then left, wanting to see Gramma. He had gone to the house when Melanie had come, staying only long enough to make sure that Tiffany wasn't in any-one's way. The reassuring words Melanie had given him, and the gentle smile, told him that she under-stood and approved.

That meant more than he liked it to.

The two-way monitor he'd had installed on the wall by his workbench beeped once. Then again.

He held down the talk button, speaking into the monitor. "Yes, Mother, what would you like?"

"I'm making tea. Do you and Tiffany want some?"

Adam glanced at his watch. Five o'clock. Just about time to quit anyhow.

"I'll be in the house as soon as I'm finished cleaning up."

Ten minutes later he was walking up the steps, Tiffany trailing along behind him with her arms full of shavings that she wanted to show her grandma.

When he bent to take her shoes off, she dropped a shaving on his head, giggling.

"You silly girl," he said, pleasure knifing through him at her spontaneous gesture.

"You are silly," she replied.

Adam held the door open for her as he took the shaving off his head, brushing excess sawdust off his pants. Tiffany stopped, then dropped her shavings on the porch floor. "Mellalie," she called out as she ran into the kitchen.

Adam looked up in surprise. Melanie, who was pouring tea for his mother, looked up, her eyes meeting and holding his.

"I have some papers I need you to sign," she said quietly, setting down the teapot. "Floyd is supposed to be here, as well. I hope you don't mind. Floyd made the arrangements with your mother."

"I'm sorry, Adam," Helen said, shooting her son

an apologetic look. "I forgot to tell you. Floyd said it should be done at his office, but I told him you could do it here."

"That's okay," Adam said, making the required noises. He wished he had known she was coming. He was suddenly aware of the sawdust coating his face and hair, the bits of wood still clinging to his pants. Melanie's pale yellow shirt and khaki pants gave her a cool elegance that made him feel grubby.

Tiffany crawled up onto Melanie's lap, exuberantly relating the events of the day, the wood shavings on her clothes brushing off on Melanie's.

"Tiffany, we should clean you up," Adam said, about to take his daughter away.

"She's fine. Just hand me a wet cloth and we can take the purple Popsicle marks off her face." Melanie smiled up at Adam, and once again he was struck by her beauty.

A beauty, he realized, that was more than the line of her features, the color of her eyes.

A beauty that radiated through her.

The other day in the cemetery he had seen another side of her. Her sorrow had added another dimension to her personality, which seemed to expand, moving slowly, inexorably into his own thoughts.

He turned abruptly away, dampened a cloth and handed it quickly to Melanie. When Adam was finished washing his hands, Melanie had wiped Tiffany's hands and face and was carefully picking bits of wood out of her hair, combing her fingers through Tiffany's tangled curls.

Adam couldn't take his eyes off the two of them.

The sight of his daughter on Melanie's lap seemed so right. Like the pieces of the drawer he had just put together, they fit.

Perfectly.

"Isn't this a nice surprise, Adam?" his mother asked, her voice fairly dripping with honey.

Caught, he thought. Staring at Melanie like some love-struck young teenager.

"Very nice," he said, sitting at the spot designated for him, avoiding his mother's knowing look. "I'm guessing the bank didn't have any problem with the estimate I gave you?" He turned his attention to Melanie, who was pouring tea again, steam wreathing between them.

Melanie waggled her fingers in a noncommittal gesture. "I had to practically give them the rights to my life in perpetuity and possibly my first child, should I ever have one, but yes. In the end, Bob said he would start the paperwork on the loan."

Adam didn't care that Floyd hadn't arrived yet. He was more than happy to sit in the kitchen of his house drinking tea with Melanie and his mother as the late-afternoon sun slanted into the kitchen.

Just like a little family.

"Hello. Sorry I'm late." Floyd's booming voice broke in to the little tableau. Adam stifled a burst of annoyance and turned to greet him.

Floyd made his way around the table shaking hands with his mother, himself and lastly Melanie.

He didn't know if it was his imagination, but did Floyd linger a little longer with Melanie, hold her hand just a little more, make just a little too much eye contact?

"So I brought the papers." Floyd pulled up a chair between Melanie and Adam, flicked open his briefcase, pulled out a set of papers and laid them on the table.

"As you can see, this is a straightforward Agreement for Sale." Floyd set his briefcase on the floor, pulled a gold pen out of his pocket and went over the details of the contract.

Adam listened with only half his attention. Instead he found himself watching Melanie, who was leaning over the agreement her eyes bright with anticipation. He knew how badly she wanted this house.

"So do you have any questions?" Floyd was asking.

"The list of assets that come with the property is laid out somewhere?" Melanie asked.

Floyd pointed them out. "Is there anything missing or anything that you wanted to add, Adam?"

Adam glanced down at the piece of paper and shook his head. Once he signed it, things would be put in motion that would remove this house and this memory from his life. He would have some more money to put into the growing construction business and one less debt to worry about.

So why wasn't he happier?

Melanie leaned past Tiffany still sitting on her lap and signed the paper with a flowing signature that looked like her, Adam thought as he took the pen from Floyd.

It was still warm from Melanie's fingers. Even a bit sticky from the Popsicle stain she'd removed.

He looked at the space he was supposed to sign, nodding when Floyd pointed it out.

Memories flitted through his mind. The endless trips he and Lana had made looking for just the right paint. Piling the lumber up in the yard in preparation for the renovations they were going to make.

Buying the shingles at an auction for a fraction of the cost, hoping they would have enough to do the entire roof.

But in each memory, Lana was just a shadowy figure.

Adam, still looking down at the paper, tried to re-create the color of her hair, the sound of her voice. But he couldn't picture her face.

"Are you okay, Adam?" Melanie asked, her voice breaking in to his thoughts.

He pulled his lower lip between his teeth, looked up at her. Felt the pull of her warmth, her gentle smile. Felt a sudden loneliness that had claws and that clung.

"You just need to put your signature here," Floyd said again, pointing a manicured finger to the line.

Adam pulled himself into the moment, looked back down at the paper and quickly scrawled his signature on the bottom just below Melanie's.

It was done and it was time to move on. If it wasn't for this house, Lana would still be alive.

He handed the pen back to Floyd. Floyd wiped it with the cloth still lying on the table, then tucked it into his pocket.

"Great stuff. So now all we have to do is wait for the financing to come through."

Adam poured sugar into his tea and stirred it absently, listening with half an ear as Melanie and Floyd's conversation moved from business to idle chitchat. Adam kept out of the conversation, ignoring his mother's attempts to draw him in.

His part of the deal was over and he had nothing to say to Floyd.

Floyd, however, had a lot to say to Melanie, amusing her with stories about local people. Floyd's business kept him in touch with a variety of people and he had a story for every person he met.

And Adam didn't like the way Melanie laughed at every story Floyd told.

You're acting like a jealous suitor, he thought, swigging down the rest of his tea. But just as he started to wonder how long Floyd was going to be entertaining them, Melanie got up and set Tiffany on the floor.

"I should be going," she said, idly brushing her hand over the little girl's hair. "Thanks so much for coming out here, Floyd. I really appreciate it."

"No problem. Glad to be of service." Floyd shook her hand. "Adam, it was a pleasure. I'll be in touch once Melanie's financing goes through." He shook Adam's hand, then Helen's. Made a general comment of farewell, patted Tiffany on the head, then gave Melanie one more smile.

Adam felt his irritation growing with each grin Floyd gave Melanie. He walked Floyd to the door, followed by Melanie and Tiffany. As they said a final round of goodbyes, Adam was fully aware of Melanie at his side. Tiffany in front of him.

Like a family.

He felt a twist of sorrow followed by an echo of a previous, equally unwelcome feeling.

Loneliness.

He wanted to be a family. It was what he and Lana had dreamed of when they bought this house. And now, with Melanie beside him, the picture was an imitation of that dream.

Yet as he glanced sidelong at Melanie, he let another dream tease him. This house. This woman.

And what about Lana?

The memory of his wife brought a clench of guilt over what might have been. She was why he was selling the house. The dream was over.

Melanie tucked her blood pressure cuff back into her nurse's bag and made a quick notation in Helen's file.

"You're frowning again. What's wrong?" Helen asked.

"I'm a little concerned about your blood pressure. Has the new medication helped any?"

"A little." Helen pulled her glasses off and polished them, her movements slow. "Adam asked if I could tell you to meet him in the shop this morning. He has something he wants to show you."

Melanie zipped her bag shut, trying to read past Helen's vague pronouncement and complacent grin.

The final sale of the house didn't seem to affect Helen at all. In spite of her blood pressure, Helen hadn't spiked a temperature for a couple of days now and she seemed more relaxed.

"Is Tiffany with him?" Melanie asked.

"She's been spending more and more time with him every day. It's wonderful to see." Helen put her glasses on. "I'm glad you talked him out of going to Disneyland. He's a good father who had to learn so many things the hard way." Helen slowly got to her feet, her bright eyes fixed on Melanie. "And now I'm just going to sit in the front room for a while. I have a book there I've been reading." She gave Melanie a wistful look. "I want to enjoy the view as long as I can. Who knows what the next month will bring? And don't look so sad," Helen said as Melanie put the walker in front of her. "I've been praying every night. And the Lord moves in mysterious ways."

Melanie wasn't even going to ask what Helen's prayers consisted of. It was no surprise to Melanie that Adam retreated to his shop as soon as she came each day. The heavy-handed hints Helen ladled out were enough to make Melanie blush. She didn't want to know what Adam thought.

"Mysterious indeed," Melanie murmured. "I'll stop in before I leave, though. Just to see if you need anything."

"Take your time," Helen said with a conspiratorial wink.

Melanie stopped at her car and set her bag inside before she went to the shop. As she closed the door, she looked around the yard once more. In a month or so this place was going to be hers.

Her first home.

Melanie took her time walking to the shop at the back of the lot, trying to absorb this wonderful actuality. Displacing Helen was the only lingering melancholy.

And what about the son and granddaughter?

Melanie dismissed the errant thought as she knocked lightly on the shop door and pushed it open. Adam had his own plans.

Tiffany looked up and jumped to her feet, scattering the rough wooden blocks she was playing with.

"Mellalie, you are here," she called out, running to her.

Adam stood at the workbench with his back to her, but turned as she closed the door.

It took a moment for Melanie's eyes to adjust from the bright natural sunlight to the artificial lighting in the shop. But in spite of that, she easily caught Adam's gaze with her own.

"Helen said you wanted to see me?" she asked, taking a slow sniff of the wood scent that permeated the shop. "It smells good in here."

Adam smiled at her, leaning back against his workbench. "Brings back memories, that's for sure."

"Memories?" Melanie prompted.

"I used to work with Lana's father building houses and cabinets." He brushed sawdust off his arms as if doing the same with his past as he pushed himself away from the bench. "I've got something for you."

Curious, Melanie followed him to the other side of the shop to a window where a faded blanket shrouded a tall shape.

"I managed to salvage what I could and reuse it,"

he was saying as he pulled the blanket away. "I tried to follow the same dimensions and pattern, but couldn't match the stain."

He stepped away, dropping the blanket on the ground and revealing a dresser.

It was the dresser he had broken.

"You fixed it," she said with a sense of wonder. She came up beside him. But as she touched it she heard his previous words again and realized what he had done.

"This isn't the old dresser." She pulled open the drawers one at a time, releasing the sharp scent of freshly cut wood. She looked at him, trying to understand. "You built this? From scratch?"

"Pine, actually," he said with a faint grin. A dimple dented one cheek. "I used the same pulls, but I had to sand the rust off a few of them." He pulled out one of the drawers and set it on its side on the blanket. "I took a few liberties with the design. The original didn't have dovetail joints, but it makes for a stronger drawer if you do that."

Something hard and bright flashed within her as he spoke. He had made this beautiful piece of furniture. Had spent all this time replacing something she had yearned only briefly for. Had done all this.

Politeness deemed that she protest. But she couldn't speak words she didn't feel. Adam had made this. His hands had crafted it. As he pointed out other things he had done, his hands touching the silky-smooth wood, Melanie caught an undercurrent of the pride of a craftsman.

She touched the dresser again, trying to assimilate

the emotions that threatened to overwhelm her. He had spent hours on this. For her.

"It's beautiful." She slid her hands over the surface, tracing the grain of the wood enhanced by the stain, deepened by the varnish. Even to her untrained eye, she could see that Adam had a gift. Each drawer slid smoothly in and out, their panels so well aligned not a gap showed between them. "I can't believe you did this."

"I'm glad you like it. I enjoyed making it."

She walked around it, still touching it, overcome by a sense of wonder and amazement. She stopped in front of him. "This is the most amazing gift I've ever received."

"Surely you've received gifts before. From your parents."

Melanie swallowed an unexpected knot of emotion. "My father, when he remembered my birthday, always sent money and my mother gave me more practical gifts. No one has ever done anything like this."

She lowered her head, blinking at the moisture welling in her eyes, swallowing against the thickness in her throat.

Adam laid a rough fingertip along her cheek and gently urged her to look up at him.

"I'm glad you like it," he said, his voice low, a soft smile curving his fine lips.

"It's beautiful." She gave in to an impulse and threw her arms around his neck. It was supposed to be a quick hug. A thank-you for something that deserved more than just words.

But as she drew away her hands lingered on the

curls of hair at his neck, then rested on his shoulders. He held her by the arms, his fingers rough against her skin, his fingertips lightly massaging her upper arms. Their eyes met and held, a connection almost physical in intensity.

Her flighty pulse stepped up its shallow rhythm. Melanie let her hands slide down his arms as she fought to regain the breath she'd lost. She wanted to move away.

She wanted to be drawn into his arms.

She hesitated, lost in the confused back-and-forth of longing and reality.

His hands lingered on her arms, then he released her.

"Mellalie, come and see my tower."

Melanie swallowed again, sucked in a deep breath, willing her pounding heart to steady as she turned to the little girl who had been playing happily at their feet, oblivious to what had just happened.

"It's very nice," Melanie said automatically. She helped Tiffany place another block on the tower, her hands unsteady and trembling. And what had happened? Nothing. You were just a little overexuberant in your thanks, she reminded herself as she drew in another breath.

"I was wondering if you want me to move the dresser to the house," Adam was saying behind her. "But if you prefer I can bring it to your apartment."

Melanie drew in another breath and turned back to the dresser, touching it again rather than looking at Adam. "Though I'd love to have it in my apartment, it seems a shame to move it all the way to my house when it's just going to come back here.''

''I'll move it to Donna's room if you want.''

''That would be great. I can go up and look at it each time I come.'' She granted him an amiable smile. ''I wish I knew how to thank you.''

''No thanks necessary,'' Adam said.

Melanie once again touched the dresser, its finish silky smooth. ''I'm overwhelmed. I will say it's the most wonderful thing I've ever received. I feel quite unworthy. I don't know what to say.''

''You seem to be doing okay,'' he said with a light teasing tone, as if the moment they had shared hadn't happened.

Melanie drew in a steadying breath. Maybe nothing had happened. Maybe it was just her own silly day-dreams and yearnings getting mixed up in this attractive man that had created that moment of awareness.

But as she drove away, she couldn't help but look back. And notice Adam standing in the doorway of his shop, watching her. He was smiling.

Chapter Eight

"I hear that Adam wants to move Helen to Calgary fairly soon." Dr. Leon Drew slipped his hands into the pockets of his lab coat and leaned back against his desk. Melanie had stopped by Dr. Drew's office to ask him about one of his patients. "What's your take on that?"

"It's complicated. Helen wants me to convince Adam to let her stay. Adam wants me to convince Helen to go. I think Adam is resigned to staying for at least another week."

"Adam Engler has had a lot to deal with in the past few years," Leon said quietly. "I don't blame him for wanting to see that his mother is okay."

It was the tone of his voice rather than his words that made Melanie stop. "You're talking about Lana?"

Leon nodded. "Losing her must have been hard. I often wondered if that was why he moved away."

"I don't think he's gotten over it."

"She was such a puzzle to me," Leon continued, looking beyond Melanie, as if looking into the past. "When she was first diagnosed as diabetic, she was fourteen. She would argue with me constantly. Over her blood sugars, her ketone levels, her diet." Leon sighed. "It took her a while to settle down. I'm still surprised she went into shock. I thought she had finally accepted her diabetes."

"Adam seems to think she died because their home was so far from the hospital."

Leon Drew shrugged. "That could have been a factor. But if she was balanced, it wouldn't have been. She wouldn't have gone out of control so fast."

"What do you mean, 'if'? Didn't you know?"

"I wasn't her doctor when she got pregnant. She was seeing a lady doctor in Eastbar, who apparently was a diabetic, as well." Leon pushed himself away from the desk. "I better get going myself. I promised my wife I'd be home on time for supper tonight and my day falls apart real quick these days. Say hello to Helen for me."

"I'll do that." Melanie slipped her briefcase over her shoulder, sifting the information Leon had given her and trying to put it together with what Adam had told her.

Something didn't quite fit, and it bothered her.

Adam pulled into an empty spot beside a small sports car that looked exactly like Melanie's.

He tapped his fingers on the steering wheel, looking out across the park. People were clumped up in groups talking, kids tearing around. The sun shone benevolently over the small town scene like a benediction.

Was this really such a good idea? He'd been out of touch with so many people it was almost an embarrassment to suddenly show up at a community function.

"Go out and play?" Tiffany asked, leaning forward in her car seat.

He sighed lightly, smiling at the eagerness on his daughter's face. It was for her that he did this, he reminded himself as he got out of the truck.

"C'mon, sweetheart, let's go see if anyone even remembers who we are." He unbuckled his daughter and lifted her out of the seat.

He settled her in his arms, took a deep breath and walked toward the groups of people.

"Good afternoon. Glad you could come." A tall, elegant-looking woman spotted them and walked toward them, her strappy sandals an incongruity on the grass. She frowned as she came nearer, then held out her hands in welcome. "I can't believe it. Adam Engler. Hello. I'm Serena Davis." She spoke the name with a gentle questioning tone. As if he should remember her.

"Hello, Serena." Adam kept the frown he felt from showing.

"You don't remember me, do you?" Serena pouted lightly. "We went to high school together. We had Mrs. Hunter for English 10."

Adam lifted his shoulder in a vague gesture. "I'm sorry."

Serena waved his apology away. "I was only

around for a couple of years, then I moved away. From what I remember you were probably too busy with hockey and volleyball."

And Lana.

Her name wasn't spoken, but Adam sensed that Serena had thought it. The sympathetic look she gave him confirmed it.

"Anyhow, come and meet the rest of the people," Serena said, turning.

And suddenly Melanie was there.

She wore a bright orange shirt over a khaki-colored skirt, her dark hair framing her face like a halo.

"Hey, Mel," Serena said, tucking her arm in Melanie's. "I'm guessing you came to say hello to Adam."

Melanie directed a careful smile his way. "Your mom decided to stay home?"

Adam nodded, shifting Tiffany on his hip. "She had a bunch of women over, and I had some shopping to do. So I thought me and Tiffany would stop by."

"I'm glad you did."

A gentle silence drifted up between them, an echo of the moment in the shop.

"Well, I've got to run." Serena patted Tiffany on the arm, giving Adam one more lingering glance. "I'm sure you can take care of him," she said to Melanie. "Don't forget to kiss Janey's baby."

"As long as I don't have to change the diaper," Melanie replied.

"Who is Janey?" Adam asked when Serena was gone.

"One of the secretaries at work. She just had a

baby. Do you want some punch? They've got some bowls set up by the pavilion.''

"Sure. I guess we may as well start mingling.''

"You'll do just fine,'' she said with an encouraging smile.

Adam took a deep breath, glancing over the crowd, and followed her. They didn't get far.

"Melanie, so glad you came.'' A plump older woman stopped the little group, smiling at Melanie, glancing over at Adam.

"Adam, this is Lois Tessier, a co-worker of mine,'' Melanie said, introducing the woman.

"And Bob's mother, don't forget.'' Lois winked at Melanie. Her perfunctory handshake told Adam exactly what Lois thought of his presence. "Bob was hoping you'd come. He's probably talking golf with his buddies, but I can tell him you're here.''

Melanie shifted her stance, putting her slightly closer to Adam. Her body language was eloquent and for a moment he was tempted to put his arm around her. Draw her close as if claiming her.

"So my loans officer plays golf. I'll have to remember that,'' she said with a bright smile. "But I should go and say hello to a few more people. Talk to you later.''

As they walked away, Adam said, "I didn't know you were interested in golf.''

"I'm not. But now I know why I won't be starting.'' Melanie angled him a quick smile, coupled with a mischievous twinkle.

"Hey, stranger.''

A hand dropped on his shoulder and Adam turned

to the familiar voice. Tall, blond hair worn overly long, mustache and a beard. "Where have you been?" he asked.

Recognition swept away his hesitancy about coming to this picnic. "Hey, Graydon. I see you still haven't found a decent barber." Adam grinned at his former co-worker and old friend with a warmth he hadn't felt since arriving back in Derwin. Graydon had been the only friend of his who had taken the time to come and see him in Calgary from time to time.

Graydon Magrath gave Adam's shoulder a quick shake. "I can't believe you haven't had time to look up your old buddies. Mr. Gerrard was just asking about you the other day. Didn't even know you were around."

"I haven't been back that long," Adam said, clapping his hand on Graydon's. "Been busy at the house, taking care of my mom. Been meaning to call you and catch up."

"I heard about her hurting herself. How's she doing?"

"Not too bad." He turned to Melanie. "You could ask my mom's nurse, Melanie Visser. She would know better."

"I know this delightful woman," Graydon said, winking at Melanie. "I see her around, but when I try to say hi in town, she won't give me the time of day."

"I'd say hi if I met you on the sidewalk." Melanie's tone was wry, but a smile hovered over her mouth. "When I hear someone whistling from their truck, I usually assume they are high school students saying hey to their friends.''

Graydon just grinned, slapping his hand on his chest. ''That's me. The world's oldest teenager.'' Graydon turned to Adam. ''You got a feisty one in her.''

Adam didn't like the inference Graydon made, but didn't bother to correct him. He suspected that three years hadn't caused much change in his friend. Graydon was always the cliché construction worker.

''So you gonna settle down now, strap on your pouch and come back to work for me now that I'm Gerrard's partner? It'd be like old times.'' Graydon set his hands on his hips as if he was ready to swing a hammer right that moment.

''You bought out half the business?'' This was news indeed.

''He said he wants to keep working but not as hard as he used to. He hasn't been the same since...'' Graydon stopped, biting his lip. ''Anyway, he said he was getting too old to run after bills and lazy framers. Said I could do that part.''

Adam chose to skip over Graydon's slip. He knew what Tom Gerrard felt. ''Actually I'm pulling up my last root,'' he said with false heartiness. ''The house is for sale. I'm taking my mother back to Calgary.''

''What? That great house?'' Graydon lowered his hands. Frowned. ''Why'd you want to do that? I always thought you'd come back to your senses and settle down here. And looks like you've got a good start.'' He looked at Melanie, then back at Adam as if expecting Adam to make a further announcement.

"Melanie is buying my house."

Graydon's disappointment clearly showed in his lugubrious expression.

"I've got a good business going in Calgary," Adam hastened to explain, convincing his friend and himself. "I'm making good money. I've been there three years already. I'm practically settled in there." And in a few weeks his mother would be, as well.

Graydon huffed his disapproval. "Three years is way too long to be building those lousy office buildings and warehouses. No personality in them. No care. You had such a good touch. Why waste it on glass and metal?"

Graydon's words struck too close to the feelings Adam had experienced before. But what could he do? There was no way he could settle back here.

His friend turned to Melanie as if appealing to her to make Adam change his mind. "This man was born to be a fine woodworker. You should see the work this man does. The things he can make wood do. It'd make me cry if I was a woman." Graydon pretended to wipe his eyes. "I get a little weepy just thinking about the waste of God-given talent."

"Actually I have seen what Adam can do with wood," Melanie said, turning to Adam. "And you're right." Melanie didn't state which one of Graydon's outrageous statements she concurred with, but Adam remembered the glint of tears in her eyes when she'd seen the dresser. Her tremulous voice as she thanked him.

He smiled back at her, and the emotion of that moment reverberated between them as strongly as a touch.

"Hey, Graydon. We need you at the barbecue," someone called out across the yard.

"Be right there," Graydon's voice boomed back.

"Okay. I'm going to go fry some steaks," Graydon said loudly, taking a couple of steps back as if giving them space. "You two just carry on. Adam, you owe me about ten hours of conversation and catching up, so I'm gonna get you later."

"More like twenty hours," Adam said with a forced grin, searching for the casual give-and-take he and Graydon always shared. "We'll talk. For sure."

Graydon pointed a finger at him. "It's a deal." He winked at Melanie. "You try to convince him he should stay. Maybe you could find a room in that house for him. And his little girl."

Adam stifled his impatience with his friend's obvious hints. Waited until Graydon was out of earshot before turning to Melanie. "I'm sorry about that. Graydon is one of those bluff, hearty men you see in heavy truck commercials. He's just a lot of talk, but he's got a good heart."

"I know Graydon Magrath," Melanie said with a gentle smile. "I know that he's been taking care of his sister for the past six months."

Adam frowned. "What do you mean, taking care of his sister?"

"Tesha hurt both her arms in a freak accident six months ago at her job. I've been there a couple of times to arrange for home-care relief. Graydon comes every day to help her with her physiotherapy. He's got a heart as big as his voice.''

Adam felt a thrust of guilt. It had been over six months since he had seen Graydon. He'd been so caught up in his own problems that he couldn't even take the time to find out how his old friend was doing. ''I didn't know that,'' he said quietly.

''It's not something you get on the phone about.''

But Adam couldn't shake off the reality that he'd done wrong by his old friend.

''Let's go get some punch.'' Melanie touched his arm, as if reassuring him. He gave her a quick smile, thankful for her presence, yet ashamed that she had seen this part of him, as well.

As they moved through the crowd, Adam was stopped again and again, greeted by people he had done work for at one time or had known from his youth. Each conversation, each familiar face was like another gentle barb, hooking into him, pulling him further and further into life in Derwin. A life he had tried to outrun and forget.

Melanie was gracious and charming, ignoring the overt comments and smiling away the curious glances. Everyone got a personal greeting and, in many cases, a light hand on their arm as she asked a few questions about a relative or friend.

They made their way to Janey, who was holding court under a grove of poplar trees, surrounded by a variety of women, none of whom Adam recognized.

Melanie made the appropriate noises about the baby and asked the right questions. When Janey offered to let her hold the baby, Melanie took the tiny bundle of humanity easily, then squatted down to let Tiffany have a close look.

"Baby is cute," Tiffany said loudly, then pulled him closer to give him a kiss.

Adam was about to reach out and stop Tiffany, but Melanie deftly moved the infant aside, at the same time pulling Tiffany to her side to show her from another angle. "The baby is sleeping now, Tiffany," she said softly. Melanie quietly pointed out the baby's eyes, ears, carefully pulled out a diminutive hand and showed Tiffany the baby's fingers, his nails like four tiny beads.

As Adam watched, an older memory surfaced. Tiffany as a baby being held by the woman he'd hired as a nanny. The woman had tried to get him to hold his daughter, but he was afraid. She was so small, so fragile.

Besides, he had told her abruptly, covering up his own fear and loneliness, he was too busy.

Tiffany was now three times the baby's size, talking and walking and growing more independent each day.

He had missed all the steps between the brand-new baby that Melanie held in her arms and the child that Tiffany was now. Regret for those lost years clawed at him. In his rush to outrun his guilt, he had missed those first amazing years of his own daughter's life.

He would make it up to her, he promised himself. Somehow, Lord willing, he would make it up to her.

"Supper is served," Graydon called out from the smoking line of barbecues beside the park's gazebo.

"Guess I should give the baby back, shouldn't I?" Melanie said to Tiffany, slowly getting up.

"I want the baby."

Tiffany was about to grab a corner of the baby's blankets, but Adam caught her hand just in time.

"The baby needs to sleep, Tiffany," he said quietly, squatting down to look at her.

Please don't let her make a scene, he thought, holding her hand and her gaze. Not in front of these people. I know I'm not the best father, but please don't let everyone else know.

Tiffany tugged on her hand once more, but Adam held firm. Then, to his utter amazement, she suddenly stopped.

Relief came in an uplifting rush. Adam smiled at her, and stroked her cheek. "Good girl," he whispered. And as he got to his feet, she lifted her arms.

He settled her on his hip and caught Melanie's gentle smile.

"Good job," she said, touching his arm. "I think you're making progress."

He couldn't help but return her smile, hold her gaze. The moment spun out, fragile as gossamer. Adam wanted to reach out to her. Touch her.

Kiss her.

He blinked and shook his head as if to dislodge the emotions, wondering what was wrong with him.

"Let's go eat," she said lightly, turning and leading the way to the tables.

Adam followed, bemused by his reaction to her, yet unable to find a way around the unalterable facts.

She was buying his house and he was leaving a town that would never hold a place for him anymore.

"So you came here with Adam?" Graydon dropped onto the grass beside Melanie, wiping his fingers with a napkin. "That's great."

Melanie took the last bite of her bun and set the plate down beside her, carefully choosing her reply. "He and Tiffany came on their own. I just happened to meet them at the parking lot."

"*Just* happened?" Graydon's bushy eyebrows disappeared into his hair. "And then you guys sit here all cozy eating supper together. What a cute picture."

Melanie took extra care brushing the crumbs off her pants. She didn't know how to answer that without sounding defensive or flirtatious. So she chose discretion and said nothing.

"I mean, that's okay," Graydon hastened to explain, balling up the napkin and pitching it with a quick snap into a nearby garbage can. "If you came with him, that is." He grinned at her, resting his forearms on his knees. "It's about time Adam got over what happened. About time he started looking around again."

He left her absolutely no avenue out of this quagmire, Melanie thought with dismay. Graydon was determined to think that she and Adam were an item when all they really were was temporary business partners. So she said nothing.

"Oh, boy. I didn't think she would come." Graydon's arms fell as he sat up straighter, his eyes narrowed.

Melanie followed the direction of his gaze, puzzled at his sudden change of subject.

Adam stood in profile to them, holding Tiffany's hand. A young woman faced him, her hand on his shoulder. She looked to be in her mid-twenties, slim and petite with long blond hair.

"Who is she?" Melanie asked, striving to keep her voice light and vaguely interested instead of avidly curious.

"Lana's sister, Sandy. She lives in Edmonton. Must be visiting her parents, but what is she doing way out here?"

"Her parents live in Eastbar?"

Graydon angled her a curious glance. Nodded. "And how do you know that?"

Melanie shrugged away his regard, her eyes on Sandy and Adam. "I just know."

Sandy stroked Adam's arm with a proprietary air, then she slipped her arms around him, her head on his shoulder. He patted her awkwardly on the back, his other hand still in Tiffany's.

"Friendly town," Melanie murmured with a flicker of jealousy. "Adam seems to have that effect on a lot of women," she said, remembering Roxanne's exuberant greeting in the park.

And their own embrace yesterday.

"Sandy and Adam are old friends."

"Of course they are." And why should you care? In spite of that hug, the two of you don't have a future.

Sandy drew away from Adam, her expression earnest as she spoke. Adam nodded, looking down at the ground, poking it with the toe of his boot.

"I should go and talk to Mrs. Hamstead," Melanie said, pushing herself to her feet. She knew she should do something, anything, rather than watch and wonder at Adam's relationship with his former sister-in-law.

"I wouldn't worry about her," Graydon said with a wink. "Adam never felt that way about her."

"That vague pronouncement makes me feel a lot better." Melanie flashed him a quick smile, then walked toward a group of women sitting in lawn chairs.

She wasn't going to look over her shoulder. She didn't care whom Adam talked to.

In spite of her personal pep talk, just before she reached the group of women she couldn't stop a quick glance over her shoulder.

Adam was leaving.

She turned, watching as he strode through the park, Tiffany settled on his hip. He disappeared behind a group of people, then reappeared beside his truck, opening the side door to put Tiffany in her car seat. But just before he closed the door, he looked her way.

Even across the distance Melanie felt a frisson of awareness. Felt the intensity of his blue, blue eyes.

Then he got into his truck and left.

Chapter Nine

The box was just plain cardboard. Dented in the sides and held together with an elastic.

But since he and Melanie had found it, Adam hadn't been able to get it off his mind. He had set it on the workbench in his shop when he took the dresser apart and each time he worked on Melanie's dresser, the box lay as a quiet reminder, its mystery growing each day.

In this day and age of telephones and e-mail, what would have driven Jason Shewchuk to write twenty letters without a reply?

He dragged the box across his workbench and brushed off the accumulated sawdust, slipped the elastic off, then carefully lifted the lid and pulled out one of the opened letters.

He ran his fingers along the jagged edge, where it had been opened. Then, ignoring second thoughts, he pulled the letter out.

"My dear Donna," it began. "Please don't rip up

this letter. Please let me know you got it. I want you to forgive me. I want us to be a family again. I was wrong to leave, but you are wrong to push me away like this. I've tried to call you, but there is never any answer. Please, please call me.'' And underneath his signature were two telephone numbers and an address.

And that was it. A simple letter, only one page, a few lines, yet in it Adam read regret and sorrow and a longing to make a broken family whole.

Had Donna replied?

He took out the second opened letter and got his answer.

''Dear Donna, I still haven't heard anything from you. Don't push me away because of one mistake. I was wrong to blame you. Very wrong. My life is empty without you and the children. There's nothing. I want to come back, but I want you to let me know that I can.''

Adam stopped reading, feeling like an intruder into a very private grief. He carefully folded the letter, slipping it back into the envelope.

Why had Donna ignored this outpouring of sorrow? Why could she not hear what this man was saying?

He thought again of the renters who had been living in the house. They had obviously saved the letters. Why hadn't they forwarded them on?

Mystery upon mystery.

He remembered telling Melanie that Donna might not like what was in them. He could simply throw them away and be done with it.

But the cry of this man's heart, the love he professed for his wife, his children—Adam couldn't walk away from that without making sure, beyond a doubt, that Donna had heard it, too.

He picked up the box and walked to the house, glancing at his watch as he did. Melanie wasn't coming until later today, so he was okay for now.

He wasn't really avoiding her, he told himself. Just giving them both space. Going to the community picnic had been a mistake. Spending time with Melanie at that same picnic had compounded that mistake. And seeing Sandy again had underlined it. The Derwin grapevine was thriving—his mother had heard about it the next morning. Thankfully she didn't press him for more information about either Sandy or Melanie.

Helen sat in the living room, reading to Tiffany. It sounded as if they were in the very beginning of Tiffany's favorite story. They would be occupied for a while.

He set the box of letters in front of him both for inspiration and encouragement. He had Jason's last address. If he still lived there, it wouldn't be too hard to contact him.

Jason didn't live there anymore, but the person who answered the phone knew where he lived and gave him the new number. When Adam dialed it he got an answering machine. He declined to leave a message. What could he say?

But that contact was at least made. Now to get hold of Donna, and he knew where to start with that, too. It took him a few phone calls to get his friend's cell phone number.

"Graydon. How are you?" Adam tried not to sound overly hearty. He had promised Graydon they would catch up, and his hasty exit from the picnic hardly attested to that fact.

"I'm great, man," Graydon said. "Why'd you leave early? Was looking for you."

Adam hooked a kitchen chair with his foot and dropped into it. "Just had to, Graydon." It was all he could say. Seeing Lana's sister had been unexpected and harder to deal with than he'd thought. Leaving the picnic so abruptly was rude, and Graydon wasn't the only one he had to apologize to.

"Sorry I didn't come to say goodbye," he said now.

"I wasn't the only one who missed you. Melanie was walking around with a fake smile the rest of the afternoon."

Graydon's words gave one more twist to the shard of guilt, yet at the same time gave his heart a peculiar lift.

"She's a wonderful person, Adam. Deserves a wonderful man."

And that was precisely why he had left the picnic, Adam thought with dismay.

He remembered what Melanie had said about Graydon's sister, and this time asked about her. Their conversation eased some of his guilt.

"I have a question for you about Donna Shewchuk," Adam said after a while. "She's been away from here for some time. Do you have any idea how to get hold of her?"

Graydon paused, and Adam could almost picture

him twisting one of the ends of his mustache as he always did when he was thinking. "Try Nadine Fletcher, at the paper. Donna used to work there. Why?"

"I found something in the attic that belongs to her. Thought she might want it back."

"Good of you, man. But then you always were a good man. Don't be such a stranger, eh?"

"I'll be in touch." That was a promise he intended to keep, he thought, hanging up the phone. Seeing Graydon was a stark reminder of what he'd once had in this community and what he had lost by burying himself in Calgary. He had missed his good friend. The ease of his company and the history they had shared. Something he knew he and Kyle could never have.

He flipped through the phone book and found the number of the *Derwin Times*. He dialed it and was soon put through to Nadine Fletcher, whom Donna used to work for.

Adam took a pen and scribbled down the number Nadine provided, relief flowing through him. Donna was near Eastbar, which was only half an hour's drive away.

He chatted a moment with Nadine, exchanging a few pleasantries, then hung up, grinning at the number. Melanie would be so pleased.

"Thank you," he breathed. Then stopped. Who was he thanking, anyhow? God?

Melanie smoothed her hand over her skirt, adjusted the collar of her favorite red shirt and took a deep breath. *Please Lord, don't let me make a fool of myself in front of Adam,* she prayed as she got out of her car. Instead she focused on the house.

Her house.

She had spent most of last night looking over paint chips and poring over magazines trying to choose the exterior color and the trim. She had finally decided on a pale butter-yellow for the main color, sage-green for the soffits and eaves and a slate-blue for the shutters. Trying to visualize those colors on the house in front of her made her smile. Excited, even.

She pushed open the creaking gate and walked to the back of the house, looking at it from all angles. Yes. She had chosen exactly the right colors.

She let her gaze slide over the yard. Adam had been busy. The piles of lumber were gone and it looked as if he had even mowed the overgrown lawn. Each day she came, the place looked more and more like the home she remembered.

Her excitement grew. The home that was going to be hers.

The back door was open and as she lifted her hand to knock on the door, she heard Adam talking. Her fingers curled into a fist that she pressed against her beating heart. Why was it surging against her chest at the sound of his voice?

She knew why. Knew she was being foolish.

Soon this would all be over, she promised herself, knocking sharply on the door. She would be living in her dream home and Adam would be out of her life.

"Hey, Melanie. I'm glad you're here." Adam was opening the door, smiling that crooked smile of his.

A smile that made her disobedient heart start up again.

Just a chemical reaction, she reminded herself, smiling back at him. "Why? Is your mom causing you trouble again?"

Helen was finally able to try walking a few steps without her walker. The last time Melanie had come, Helen had secretly told her that Adam was constantly hovering, worried that she would hurt herself again. Though Helen had acted frustrated, Melanie could easily hear in Helen's voice the pleasure at Adam's concern.

"No. She's doing just fine." Adam stepped back, letting Melanie come into the house. "I have some great news."

Melanie set her bag on the chair, willing her heart to stop its erratic beating as she turned to him. What could he be so pleased about? Was he going to stay?

Whoa, Melanie. You are really jumping ahead. "And what is that?" she asked quietly.

Adam caught her by the arms, grinning like a kid. "I finally contacted Donna. I told her about the letters. She hadn't known anything about them."

Emotions tumbled through her, a kaleidoscope of pleasure and hope edged with a faint disappointment that Adam's news had nothing to do with him.

"Where is she? Close by here? Far away? Did she say anything about Dena?" Her excitement grew with each question.

"She lives about half an hour's drive away, north of Eastbar. I asked her if I could deliver the letters to her. And she said yes. She started to cry."

Melanie felt her own eyes prickle. She looked away. This was the second time she'd felt all teary eyed in front of Adam.

"Hey, Melanie. Are you okay?" His hands were still on her arms, his voice quiet, intimate.

"I am," she whispered. "I'm just feeling a little sentimental, that's all." And a little confused.

She wished he wasn't standing so close to her, wasn't touching her. All she would have to do was turn just a half turn, lean a few degrees ahead and she would be in his arms. Again.

The thought was far too appealing, and she carefully pulled away.

"When are you going?" she asked, her voice a little shaky.

"Tomorrow." He was quiet a moment. "Do you want to come? I can wait until you're done work."

Say no, the practical part of her urged. She could easily get the directions and go on her own.

But she wanted to be there when Donna got the letters it seemed she had never seen. She wanted to know firsthand what had happened to the family she had idealized for so long.

"I'd love to come," she said softly, her smile tremulous. "I'd love to see her again."

"Great. I'll pick you up after work."

She heard a scampering sound coming from the front room, then, "Mellalie is here."

Then the sound of running feet and Tiffany launched herself at Melanie. "You are here again," Tiffany said, grabbing Melanie's hand and dancing around her. "Come, see Gramma. You come, too."

Tiffany grabbed her father's hand, and over the top of her head Melanie caught Adam's smile.

"Looks like things are improving in the daughter department," she said quietly as they walked to the front room.

Adam nodded. "My partner wasn't happy with your advice, but it seems to be working." His smile deepened, creasing his cheeks. "We've got a bit of a ways to go, but there's definite progress. Thanks again."

His smile warmed her, and his words of thanks gave her a gentle shiver.

"I have to show you something, Melanie," Helen was saying.

With a guilty start, Melanie turned to her patient.

Then Adam left and Tiffany went with him without one word of protest. Melanie knew she should be pleased that father and daughter were slowly bonding again. But she wouldn't be honest if she didn't admit that the mothering part of her felt a tiny bit jealous.

Pink shirt okay? Did it match the pants?

Should she wear her hair up? Down? Was she wearing too much makeup? What about the perfume? Too obvious?

Melanie dragged her hair back from her face and blew out a frustrated sigh at her muted reflection in a bathroom mirror still foggy from her shower. "It's just a visit to an old friend," she said aloud, as if speaking made the reality more mundane.

But she knew it was the fact that she was going with Adam that put the flush in her cheeks and the fluttering nerves in her stomach. And created all these indecisions.

She wiped the mirror with her elbow and stood back, inspecting herself critically. She had applied the mascara with a light hand, and the eyeshadow was barely there, just as her mother had taught her.

She remembered her father teasing her mother about the makeup lessons. *Why bother putting it on at all if it's not supposed to be noticeable?* he had said as her mother was getting ready to go to church.

And he'd stayed behind.

Melanie clutched her stomach. *Dear Lord, what am I doing?* she prayed. *I'm starting down the same path my mother went. This can't be what You want for me.*

She remembered Adam's words when they'd been alone in the turret, but his words seemed less a rebellion against God than the cry of a wounded heart. A hurting soul who didn't know where to go anymore.

"You're looking for excuses," she said aloud. Firmly, as if convincing herself. Adam was coming for her and she was going to meet an old friend. Nothing more.

She flicked off the light and left the room.

Her sweater hung over the back of her kitchen chair and as she slipped it on, she gave the apartment a critical once-over. The kitchen counter, though faded and scarred, was tidy, the dishwasher swishing through its cycle. She straightened the candleholder on the kitchen table, brushed an errant crumb off its wooden surface.

She walked into the living room, picked up a magazine that lay crooked on a side table and straightened a few books on the bookshelf.

A tall book sat between two short books. She was about to pull it out and move it, then stopped.

Fussy old maid, she thought. What are you going to be like when you get the house?

A sudden sorrow, so familiar it felt like a friend, clenched her midsection. She looked around her apartment again.

What was a single woman like her doing buying a house in a small town like Derwin? Was she pinning too much on an old dream she couldn't let go of?

The intercom buzzer sounded, saving her from her roiling thoughts. Adam.

Her heart danced.

"Be right down," she said into the speaker.

She didn't give him a chance to answer, but caught her purse from the hook beside her door, locked the door and ran down the stairs.

He stood in the entrance frowning at the speaker, as if it had let him down, his hands in the pockets of his ever-present blue jeans. These were clean and pressed and the white shirt tucked into them was a bright contrast against his tanned skin.

His sandy hair was brushed, a few curls already springing up around his ears and over the collar of his shirt. Then he turned, saw her and his smile broke free.

Melanie couldn't stop the answering quaver of her errant heart or her own lips as they curved up in response.

She opened the door and for a moment they stood

facing each other, each saying nothing, awareness arching between them.

Melanie was the first to look away, her prayer of a few moments ago slowly seeping back, bringing with it a gentle peace. *Lord, work Your will in my life,* Melanie prayed as she stepped past Adam. *And work in Adam's life, as well. Let him feel Your love. Your forgiveness.*

By praying for him, it was as if she dismantled the miscreant hold he had on her emotions. He was a lonely soul in need of God's love. And in need of her prayers.

"Ready to go?" Adam asked as he pulled the outer door open for her.

"Where's Tiffany?"

"Mom's neighbor was over and offered to stay." Adam let the door fall behind him.

"I have to tell you, I'm a little nervous," she confessed, thankful for the equilibrium her prayer had given her. "I don't know what to expect. Are you sure she won't mind if I come along?"

Adam shook his head as he fished his truck keys out of his pocket. "I told her you'd be coming. Donna was really excited about seeing you. She said that she always enjoyed having you around."

Adam followed Melanie around to her side of the truck and opened the door for her. According to numerous articles in women's magazines Melanie should have felt slightly offended. Especially because she'd been living on her own for some time.

But she appreciated the small courtesy. It made her feel valued. As a single woman she did so much for herself, she didn't mind having something done for her, even if it was as minor as having a door opened.

Adam got into the truck, but before he started it, he turned to Melanie, tapping his fingers on the steering wheel. "Before we go, I know I have to apologize for leaving you so suddenly at the picnic." He paused, his teeth worrying his lower lip. "I should have said something yesterday, but somehow I just couldn't find the right way to do it. Then I realized there's no right or wrong way to apologize, as long as I just do it." He looked up at her then, one corner of his mouth pulled up in a half smile. "Forgive me?"

"Of course I forgive you," she said, stifling the questions that scurried through her mind. What Adam discussed with his sister-in-law was none of her business. Though Serena had given her the background on Sandy's lifelong crush on Adam, it had no affect on her.

She gave him a quick smile, adding to her words of forgiveness, then caught sight of the box nestled in the car seat between them.

"Are these the letters?" she asked, laying her hand on the box.

Adam nodded, then started up the truck and pulled into the street. "I just hope there's nothing offensive in them. I read the opened ones and that was what made up my mind to bring them to Donna."

"Do you mind telling me what was in them?"

He said nothing for a moment, a light frown creasing his forehead. "They were the words of a man still in love with his wife. I couldn't just leave them sitting in the box. Couldn't throw them away." He gave her a quick glance and Melanie was surprised to see the pain in his eyes. She thought again of Lana and realized that though he said little about his wife, he still felt the loss.

"Does Donna know what is in them?"

"I thought it best if she read them for herself." Adam turned the truck onto the main highway leading north out of town. "I don't know how she'll react anyhow."

"I'm going to pray that she will have an open heart." Melanie knew she was taking a chance mentioning prayer, but to her surprise, Adam said nothing.

She leaned back in her seat as the buildings of the industrial park gave way to the open fields. She wasn't often a passenger, so she took the time to appreciate the countryside.

Two months ago, when Melanie had first come to Derwin, the grain in the fields had been just a faint tinge of tender green against black dirt. Now their full heads swayed and flowed in the wind. Tractors cut thick swaths in fields of hay that had been only ankle high.

In a month swathers would be working in the grain-fields, getting ready for the harvest and another season.

Summer and winter. Springtime and harvest. The seasons and the time flowed on.

This afternoon she had gone to the bank and signed another set of papers giving the bank authority to check her tax records—yet another step in the ongoing saga of trying to get financing. She hadn't heard anything about the full-time position at the clinic and though she hadn't admitted it to anyone, she was getting concerned. When she'd spoken to the supervisor at the picnic on Saturday, she had practically assured Melanie that the job was hers.

"And where are you?"

Adam's soft question brushed away her concerns. It would all come together—she was just feeling a little melancholy was all. Summer did that to her.

"Just thinking about how nice it is not to have to drive once in a while."

"Don't like driving?"

"I like to look around. Which can cause problems when I'm driving. I usually end up going slower and slower."

Adam smiled. "One of those drivers that I usually pass as soon as I can."

"Mr. Busy Contractor on his way to the next job," she said with a teasing tone in her voice. "Though I notice that you don't have your usual pile of papers on the kitchen table anymore."

"A nurse gave me some good advice about working holidays." He glanced sidelong at her, then away. "For the sake of my health, mind you."

"I'm glad you took it. Tiffany seems a lot more relaxed in your company."

"It's been an interesting time." He waved a hand her way. "We've got a long ways to go, but once we're back in Calgary, things will change."

"That's good."

Back in Calgary. Reality check once again for you, Melanie thought.

And there seemed nothing more to say after that.

Ten minutes later when Adam pulled into the short driveway of a house near Eastbar Melanie's heart quickened with a mixture of excitement and uneasiness. What was Donna like after the sorrows that life had dealt her?

The door of the house opened as Melanie got out of the truck. A woman stood in the doorway, one arm folded across her stomach in a defensive gesture, her other hand cupping her chin. Silver glinted in her dark hair. Dark eyes that had once snapped with vigor and life now held a resigned look.

Then those eyes riveted on Melanie. Held.

"Is that you, Melanie?"

"Hello, Donna." Melanie took a hesitant step toward the woman she had once thought of as her other mother.

Donna blinked, as if to register what she was seeing. Then she flew down the steps, her arms wide. "Oh, my little girl. I can't believe you're here." And Melanie was held close in a tight embrace that she returned.

It had been so long since she had been held in a mother's embrace. So long since she had been supported. Then, as if all the sorrows of the past years returned in one sudden outpouring of emotion, a sob slipped past her thickened throat and another as tears filled her eyes.

"Oh, sweetheart, what things have happened to you?" Donna murmured, still holding her close, rocking her as if to comfort her.

Melanie swallowed, took a shuddering breath and

pulled back, wiping her eyes with a trembling hand. "I'm sorry, Donna. I don't know what came over me."

Donna's eyes were shining as well, but she gently pushed Melanie's hair back from her face, smiling a motherly smile. "I think you've had your own burdens to bear." Soft brown eyes held Melanie's, sympathy and sorrow shining out of them. Donna stroked Melanie's cheek, then drew her close and kissed her lightly. "It's been too long and I'm sure we have much to talk about." She looked over Melanie's shoulder, smiling now. "And I'm presuming this is Adam."

Melanie wiped her tears away, hoping her mascara hadn't smudged, then glanced back at Adam, who stood by the truck, a bemused expression on his face.

He shook Donna's hand. "Glad to meet you face-to-face."

She clung to his hand, her eyes bright. "You said you had something for me?"

He nodded.

"Come in. Come in. You can show me there."

Just as Melanie turned to follow Donna, she felt Adam's hand behind her back, helping her along. Supporting her.

Chapter Ten

Donna held the box of letters on her lap, her finger toying nervously with the elastic. "There's how many letters in here?"

"Twenty." Adam set his mug down on the table and leaned forward, stifling the guilt he still felt at reading the letters. "The first ones were opened already."

Donna's fingers ran back and forth over the elastic. "He didn't contact me at all after he left. I waited by the phone. Checked the mail every day, but nothing came. I never knew how to contact him. How to tell him I was sorry."

"What happened, Donna?" Melanie asked. "You were always such a close family."

Donna lifted the elastic and let it go with a snap. "Do you remember Lonnie?"

"He was just a little boy when I used to come here. Your youngest," Melanie said quietly.

"He's a teenager now. He's with a friend. I didn't

want him here when you came." Donna sighed lightly. "When he was little there was a bad accident. On the property. Lonnie fell down an open well hole that hadn't been covered. He fractured his skull, broke his hip and almost drowned." Melanie gasped and Donna pressed her fingers to her lips, as if holding her own sorrow back. "He was in a coma for a month. I had been after Jason for months to get a proper cover on the well, and he told me I should have kept a better eye on Lonnie. We constantly blamed each other, then we stopped talking. For a while it looked as if Lonnie wasn't going to come out of it. Every day I would go to the hospital. Every day we would wait. Pray. The doctor wasn't optimistic, which didn't help our situation any. One day, after an especially bad day, we had a huge fight. Jason said if he was such a bad husband, such a terrible father, why didn't I just ask him to leave." Donna bit her lip. Drew in a shaky breath and gave Melanie a tremulous smile. "So I did. And he left. He'd phone the hospital to see how Lonnie was, but he never phoned here or wrote."

"How could you have sold the house if Jason was gone?" Adam asked. He didn't remember the details of the sale. Only that Donna was the only one they had dealt with.

"I got the house from my father. He didn't care for Jason. One of the conditions of getting the house was that only my name show up on the title. Which caused a lot of bitterness, as well." Donna sighed lightly, shaking her head. "But in spite of all that, we were happy until the accident. Jason was a good husband and a good provider. He never even contacted me about getting a divorce. I didn't want one, either.'' Donna sniffed and carefully wiped a few tears away. Melanie slipped her arm over Donna's shoulder.

"I have good memories of coming to your place," Melanie said. "It was always a dream of mine to have a home like yours."

"I guess you'll have to find another dream," Donna said softly. "This one is over."

Adam couldn't stand it anymore. "Don't say that. Read the letters and you'll know different."

Melanie gave him a surprised glance.

"I read the first two," he said, refusing to apologize for that. "They are a cry from a lonely heart. Please give him a listen."

Donna blinked again and then, with a decisive movement, slipped the elastic off the box. She lifted the first letter out, glancing quickly at Melanie, who nodded in encouragement.

Adam felt like a voyeur, but he wanted to see this to the end. Wanted to know that Jason would get a fair hearing.

Donna scanned the lines, her eyes flying back and forth. Then slowing. Filling. Her fingers trembled against her lips as glistening tears slid silently down her cheeks.

"What have I done?" she whispered. She put the letter down, disregarding the moisture on her cheeks. Opened the next one and read it once. Then again.

As she ripped open the third one, a cheque fluttered out to the table. Donna turned it over and closed her eyes.

"What have I done?" she repeated. Then she put her hands to her face and burst into tears.

Adam's throat tightened as he watched Donna's sorrow and regret spill over. Listened as she confessed her stubbornness to Melanie.

"You didn't know where he lived, Donna," Melanie whispered, cradling Donna close, rocking lightly. "You didn't get the letters—how could you know?"

"I didn't try very hard," Donna sobbed.

Adam felt superfluous, yet couldn't move away from this open display of honest emotion.

"Why didn't I get the letters?" she cried, swiping at her eyes with a limp hankie that Melanie had given her. "I gave the post office my change of address."

"When did you do that?" Adam asked.

Donna sniffed again. "A few months after I moved away. I just didn't think of it at the time. I just wanted to leave."

"I'm pretty sure the people renting the house were getting them and not forwarding them on." Adam leaned forward, took the envelope of the first one and set it beside the last letter, which was still unopened. "The cancellation dates of the first and the last one are only three months apart."

"I prayed and I prayed that he would contact me." Donna wiped her eyes. "I guess my prayers were answered. Sort of."

"Oh, Donna, I'm so sorry for you," Melanie said, stroking Donna's shoulder.

"Don't be," Donna said, pressing her hand against Melanie's. "I brought this on myself. I pushed him away. Did you know that many marriages break apart when a child dies or when there are problems?'' Donna said, her voice quiet. ''I used to wonder how that happened. Now I know it's because both parties get stuck in the guilt phase of grieving. The selfish part. And there's nothing left for each other and nothing left for God. If I had just forgiven Jason, let go of my own self-righteous anger, we could have helped each other grieve. And let God heal the broken parts of our lives. But I didn't know how to tell him.''

Donna's quiet words sifted into Adam's thoughts and merged with the many careful comments Melanie had made about keeping his burden of guilt to himself. Of not letting it go.

The words spun and twisted through his mind, as if trying to find entrance to a place he had blocked off.

''Now I don't even know how to contact him,'' Donna continued.

Adam pulled himself back to the moment. ''I do,'' he said, pulling a piece of paper with Jason's number out of the pocket of his blue jeans, thankful he could contribute something practical. He laid it on the table and slid it across to her.

Donna glanced at the paper and pressed it to her chest, her eyes glistening once again. ''How can I possibly thank you for what you have done?''

Adam grinned at her. ''Send me a family picture.''

''We'll see,'' Donna whispered.

''I'll be praying for you, Donna,'' Melanie said, giving Donna a hug. ''I will pray that the family I've always loved will be whole once again.''

Donna hugged her back, then reached across the

table to take Adam's hand. "Thank you again, Adam. You were my answer to prayer."

And how could that be? For many years Adam hadn't believed God answered prayer—how could he be an answer to someone else's?

Donna put the lid back on the box as if closing off that part of the evening. "Can I make you some coffee?"

"I'd like that," Melanie said, then glanced at Adam. "Unless you want to go."

He did. He wanted some quiet time, alone, to sort through the thoughts that tangled in his mind. Old emotions, regrets and thoughts came tumbling back and he didn't know where to put them. Though he tried to put God out of his life, He kept returning.

But he knew what Donna meant to Melanie, and for her sake he agreed to stay.

The conversation moved to more practical matters. Adam sat back, sipping his coffee, listening, watching as Melanie described to Donna what she wanted to do with the house, what colors she was going to paint what. Her eyes sparkled, her hands fluttered to emphasize a point, her love for the house radiating from her.

Her expression grew more serious when Donna asked about her parents. Adam's heart contracted as she described the sorrow she'd felt at her parents' breakup. Then as she spoke of the loss of her father, then her mother. Though a faint smile grazed her lips, Adam knew her well enough now to hear the reserved note of sorrow in her voice, the yearning as he realized she had no family at all.

And he understood a little more why she had spun a dream around the house.

"My goodness, I've been talking your ear off and Adam is about asleep in his chair." Melanie laughed a little self-consciously. "You should have said something, Adam."

"I didn't mind," he said with a gentle smile. "I didn't have anywhere else to be."

She held his gaze a moment, as if thanking him for his understanding, then got up.

Before they left, however, Donna gave Adam a hug. "As I said before, I don't know how to thank you," she whispered.

"Like I said, send me a family picture." He bent over and kissed her lightly on the cheek. "Take care, now."

The evening sun shed a soft light on the neighborhood as Melanie and Adam walked to his truck. The soft snick of a water sprinkler laid a gentle rhythm counterpointed by the laughter of children down the street. A young couple passed them, pushing a stroller, smiling a vague greeting as their eyes made brief contact.

It was an idyllic scene, a gentle moment, yet Adam felt a peculiar restlessness as he opened the truck door for Melanie. In the house behind them, all had not been well. He wondered about other homes on the street. How many of them held secret sorrows and pains? As he did.

"You look troubled," Melanie said as he put the truck in gear and pulled into the street.

"No, no. I'm fine." He didn't look at her.

His ambiguous answer seemed to satisfy her. When they got onto the highway, the only sound in the truck was the drone of the truck engine and the light tapping of his keys against the steering column.

The disquiet returned, relentless and unidentifiable. It was as if a crack was opening into the past, and he didn't want to go there.

Snatches of what Donna had said reverberated in his mind, pushing the crack further open—*stuck in the guilt phase of grieving…nothing left for God…let God heal the broken parts of our lives.*

And how was he supposed to do that? He had ignored God so long, how was he supposed to come back to Him?

"Where are you, Adam?"

Melanie's soft voice broke in to his reflections. He gave a guilty start. "Sorry," he said, angling her a quick glance. "I was thinking…" He let the sentence trail off. It had been so long since he'd allowed his mind to stir up old emotions and thoughts he didn't know if he could share them.

"You look sad," she continued, as if unwilling to let him pass her off.

Adam hesitated as the temptation to divulge thoughts long suppressed fought with the need to keep Melanie at arm's length. She was too appealing, too attractive. He couldn't allow himself to be distracted from his plans.

But he was tired of being strong. Tired of trying to keep a balance between what he felt and what he needed. And he was tired of holding his feelings to himself. Being at the picnic had shown him how far he had moved from community and people who cared about him.

"Guilt," he said finally.

"Over Lana's death?"

Adam nodded as familiar feelings, long buried, sifted to the surface of his mind. "It's been a while, I know, but each time I see Tiffany I think how different things could have been if only I'd listened to my own instincts."

"You take too much on," Melanie said. "Lana made choices, too."

"I know, but I don't only feel guilty when I see Tiffany. When I saw Sandy at the picnic I had to think about the Gerrards and what I took away from them, as well." Adam wrapped his hands around the steering wheel as fresh regret assaulted him.

"Maybe I'm out of line," Melanie continued, "but I wonder if it wouldn't be helpful for you to visit Lana's family."

Adam shook his head. "I'm not a part of that family anymore. Best if I just leave them be."

"But your daughter is part Gerrard."

"I let them see her. I would never take that away from Tom and Amanda. But I'm not a part of them."

"I don't think that's true."

Adam frowned at her, irritation flicking through him. She wouldn't let up. The sign for Derwin flashed by and he slowed as he took the turnoff.

He turned onto her street, the trees lining it creating a protective arch over the street and over the houses tucked back from them.

"And how do you know that Tiffany isn't the only one that counts?"

"You were married to their daughter. Surely you are a part of their life."

Adam turned into her parking lot and stopped. "I was. Once."

"What makes you think you still aren't?"

"Why are you sticking up for them?" He wrapped his hands around the steering wheel, squeezing.

"Because I think they need Tiffany, but I think they need you, too."

Adam gave a start. Looked over at her. Melanie was looking down at her thumbs, pressing them together and apart, as if she was nervous. "Why do you say that?"

Melanie dropped her hands, faced him straight on. "Maybe I don't know precisely how family works. Maybe I'm all wrong in my own assumptions, but I can't understand why you want to keep yourself apart from family of any kind."

Melanie's impassioned plea stung. Pushed aside the resistance he had built against Amanda and Tom. Against their pain.

Adam thought again of the invitation Sandy had extended to him and sighed. He wasn't going to be able to quietly leave Derwin without facing his past.

"I think you need to lay some things to rest, Adam."

"Why? I'm not staying."

But even as he spoke the words aloud, he couldn't say them with the conviction he once had. The past couple of days he had found a peace that had been missing from his life.

Working on the dresser for Melanie. Spending time with his mother and daughter.

Even taking the time to visit Donna.

None of these things would have been possible in Calgary. Kyle was pressuring him to get the money for the house to put into a project that would virtually guarantee he would be spending even less time at home than he had.

Adam looked around at the drab concrete block in front of them, the dull exterior broken up by iron balconies. Two floors up a few young boys were yelling out comments to passersby. Rap music thundered out of another window.

He felt suddenly restless and confined.

"Can we get out? I need to walk. A few blocks down, we connect up to a path that follows the river."

By the time Adam got out of the truck, Melanie was outside, waiting for him.

"You didn't even give me a chance to hold open the door for you," he said with a light smile.

"Too independent, I guess." She slipped her sweater on and buttoned it up. "You'll have to lead the way. I don't have a clue where to go."

He turned, and Melanie fell into step beside him.

"Did you grow up in town here?"

Small talk, then. That was a whole lot easier than the larger topics she wanted to discuss. "My dad had a small acreage just outside of town on the north side. It's all houses now."

"What did your father do?"

"This and that. He was a carpenter, handyman. Jack-of-all-trades and master of none was how he described himself."

"So that's where you got your carpentry skills."

Adam smiled. "When he was working in his shop, I used to spend all my spare time there, helping him. The smell of wood shavings always reminds me of him."

"How long ago did he die?"

Adam had to count back. "About four years now. He and my mother married late, so I always had older parents. I think they had more patience with me." He slipped his hands into his pockets, glancing sidelong at Melanie. They had talked enough about him. He wanted to find out more about her. "I know your mother died a while ago. What of your father?"

"He and my mother separated when I was thirteen. It wasn't the happiest of marriages."

"I heard you saying something about that to Donna. That must have been hard."

"It was almost as hard as his death." She shrugged, looking ahead, her expression pensive. "That's why Donna's family was so special to me. That's why family is important, period. You don't really know what you have until it's gone." She angled her head, the faint evening breeze teasing her hair around her face. She brushed it back and tucked it behind her ear with a casual gesture that was artlessly feminine.

His steps slowed as he looked around, simply enjoying the evening quiet, enjoying having Melanie walking alongside him. Their footfalls were muffled by the wood chips strewn on the soft ground of the path. All was peaceful, soft and gentle and his earlier restlessness drifted away.

When they came to a wooden bench overlooking the creek that danced over the stones, Adam suggested they sit down.

Melanie settled onto the bench and stretched her legs out in front of her. "I wish I'd known about this place sooner. I would have been here every day."

"My dad did some work on it—that's how I knew about it." He picked up a branch and pressed his thumbnail into the bark. Still green.

"You have quite a few roots in Derwin, don't you?"

Adam thought about the phone calls he'd made to Nadine to track Donna down. Thought about his friend Graydon. "I had good friends here."

"Good friends stay friends." Melanie angled her head toward him as a faint smile played over her lips. "I've been spending the past few days thanking you," she said quietly. "And tonight's no exception. I want to thank you so much for taking me to see Donna. For bringing her the letters. It was an answer to prayer to see her again." Melanie stopped. Her hand surreptitiously swiped at her cheek.

Another answer to prayer. Did he not do anything on his own? Were all his actions determined by the prayers of other people?

"You're welcome. It was a small thing to do." Uncomfortable with her emotions and her words, he looked back down at the stick he held. Peeled the bark away, exposing the stark white wood beneath.

She lifted her face to his, her smile full, wide. "Thank you again, Adam. You're a good person."

"I wish I could believe that." Adam stripped another piece of bark away with a jerk, tiny drops of moisture spitting out. He hadn't felt like a good person for years.

"It's true, Adam. I know you're thinking about Lana again. You have to let go of that burden. You're too caught up in her death."

"It's a reality." He dropped the stick, no longer interested in exposing its secrets. "And I have to live with the consequences."

Melanie laid her hand on his arm. "Why don't you let God heal you, bring life to those places of death? He is the God of life. He doesn't blame you for what happened. Why do you?"

He chanced a quick glance her way, and as their eyes met it was as if she drew out from him all the sorrows he had tried to bury. "Why are you doing this, Melanie? It's my past. Why are you trying to go back to it and resurrect it?"

"Because you're carrying over pain from the past and it hurts me to see that."

"Why?"

"Because I care about you," she whispered.

Her words plucked long-forgotten emotions, sending a clear note of longing singing through him.

He couldn't stop his hand from coming up. Touching her face as if underlining with a physical touch the emotional connection they shared. He traced the line of her mouth as her breath warmed his fingers.

Her skin was so soft.

Adam felt his own breath slow, felt time slip away, and he lowered his head.

As their lips met, his hand slid around her shoulders, his fingers tangled in her hair. It felt so right. So good.

She returned his kiss, her hands touching his face.

He brushed his lips over her cheek, her temple, then drew her even closer in his arms, his breath coming out in a sigh.

It was like coming home, having her in his arms. Everything that had been confusion and uncertainty slipped away, replaced by the utter rightness of holding her close to him, of feeling her hair under his chin, her arms around him.

It was as if each was afraid to break the moment with words. He stroked her hair with his chin, content to hold her close. To feel the loneliness that had clawed at him the past few years ease.

Then, far too soon, Melanie drew hesitantly back. Adam didn't let her go right away. Couldn't.

"What's happening, Adam?" Melanie asked, bringing reality back with words. "Where is this going?"

"I don't know." He stroked her cheek with his finger, relishing the fact that she allowed him, unwilling to let the reality of her questions intrude on the still, quiet place they had created.

"Are you still going to the city?"

It was as if she had pushed him into the cold water of the creek below them. Facts and reality intruded into this magical moment. Pressure and a partner who wouldn't ease off. What else could he do?

"I have to, Melanie. I can't change my plans now." He straightened. Lowered his arms.

"And God?"

Adam turned to face the creek. "I don't know where God fits into my life anymore, Melanie. I've been away so long...." Adam couldn't say anything more. Nothing in his life fit as it should. Lana had become a shadowy memory, yet the struggle with her death remained. His work was a burden he didn't want to shoulder.

And God?

Adam had spent the past few years angry at God, pushing Him away, all the while knowing he could not avoid Him.

"He's waiting. Just like Jason was waiting to hear from Donna. He still loves you and is waiting for you to let go of your struggles and your plans and your guilt."

Her words drew memories from the deep places he had buried God. A God whose love he'd once cherished. A God he trusted utterly. Whom he had turned his back on in anger and blame. He'd run so far away, how could he ever come back?

Melanie drew in a slow breath, soft as a sigh. "I don't know where this can go, Adam, if you're not sure. My mother and father broke up because he wasn't a Christian. I don't want that for myself."

Adam rested his elbows on his knees, staring at the water, wishing he knew what to say.

Then, without a backward glance, she got up and walked back to her apartment, leaving Adam confused and bereft.

Chapter Eleven

Tiffany lay curled in her bed, her fingertips resting lightly on her palms. Adam hunkered down beside the bed, resting his crossed arms beside his daughter, his eyes on her sleep-washed face, allowing himself the luxury of just watching her.

The past week had brought about a marked change in her attitude toward him, just as Melanie had predicted. And not only in her. Each day he worked around the yard he could feel the tension that usually gripped his neck and shoulders loosen a little more— and building the dresser had been pure joy.

He smiled, thinking of the satisfaction he'd felt working with the wood. Melanie's happiness when he'd given it to her.

How her arms had felt around his neck when she'd "thanked" him.

The kiss they had just shared.

He put the brakes on his wandering thoughts. That was unknown territory and, according to Melanie, unwanted. He leaned over and brushed a kiss over Tiffany's forehead. She shifted again and her eyes opened.

"Daddy," she whispered, smiling.

Adam's heart contracted with pure joy. She had called him Daddy.

In spite of his previous sorrow, her simple word made him want to pull her out of the bed and dance around the room with her.

"Hey, Tiffany," he said instead, stroking her hair. "Did you have a nice time with Gramma and the baby-sitter?"

Tiffany nodded. "You were gone? With Mellalie?"

"I was, sweetie. We had to go visit the lady who used to live in this house." He stroked her hair again, combing his fingers through its silky strands, love for his little daughter flowing through him.

"I love Mellalie," Tiffany said, shifting around in her bed. She smiled at her father once more, then her eyes drifted slowly shut.

Adam sighed lightly, his hand still tangled in his daughter's hair. He was worried about Tiffany's attachment to Melanie. What would happen when they left?

And what about your own feelings? What are you going to be thinking about when you're back in Calgary, busy every waking minute? Will you think about her then?

Do you have to go?

The question snaked into his mind and hovered.

Just this afternoon Kyle had phoned again. Had

once again pressured him to get the money from Melanie sooner. Had pushed him to come back to Calgary. They were missing a big chance, he kept saying.

Adam got tired just thinking about Kyle. These past few weeks away from him made him realize how little Kyle took Tiffany's needs into consideration. And Adam had let him.

Graydon wouldn't have done the same.

Graydon was his friend. Kyle was his partner. The work that he had done with Graydon he had been proud of. The work he did with Kyle was just another way to make money.

So which one had brought him happiness?

He pushed himself up and stood, looking down at his daughter as his confused thoughts beat in his mind like birds caught in a house.

You don't need to go back. You could stay here. With Melanie.

He closed his eyes to concentrate, to separate fact from fancy.

Melanie wanted someone who was close to God, and he didn't know how to make that step.

''Thanks, Sandy, you've been a lot of help.'' Melanie clutched the handset of the phone as Sandy's information filled in the gaps of what she already knew. After talking to Dr. Drew about Lana, Melanie had known she had to look further. Thankfully Sandy had been willing to share what she knew.

''I'll have to talk to my parents as soon as possible. Are you going to tell Adam?'' Sandy asked after a moment's pause.

"I'm going there this afternoon. But I want you to remember it's not a final analysis and it's only a theory," Melanie warned. "It's just what I've gleaned from talking to her previous doctor and the doctor in Eastbar." And now you.

"But it all fits. It doesn't change anything, and yet I think for Adam, it will change a lot."

"I hope so. And thanks so much for your help." Melanie hung up, hugging herself as she looked down at the notes sitting on her desk.

She wondered what Adam was going to make of this.

But more than that she wondered how she was going to face him after yesterday. The thought of his kiss still made her toes curl.

"You're looking dreamy." Serena dropped into a chair across from Melanie's desk. "What are you thinking about?"

Melanie picked up her pen and tapped it against the loose papers on her desk. "Nothing," she said with what she hoped was an airy tone.

"Let me rephrase that. Who were you thinking about?"

Melanie leveled a wry glance at her. "What did you come here to bother me about? I'm busy."

"Of course you are." Serena rested her chin on her hands, a patronizing smile curving her lips. "Just wondering if you've gotten your interview with the superintendent."

"I'll be seeing her Monday," Melanie said absently, making another quick note on the paper she had been scribbling on.

"You don't sound too enthused."

Melanie pulled herself to the here and now. "Sorry, my mind was elsewhere."

"Like it was a few moments ago." Serena rocked her head back and forth, grinning at her friend. "I think you're in love with Adam Engler."

Melanie's heart skipped in her chest, but she didn't deign to answer her friend. Instead she gathered up her papers with slightly shaky hands and slipped them into her briefcase. "I think you're delusional. There's help for people like you." She flashed Serena a smile, hoping she looked and sounded casual enough.

Serena just laughed. "But there's not much help for you, Melanie. You're too far gone."

Melanie just waved over her shoulder. Serena's comments had hit too close and she didn't want to give her any more ammunition to work with.

"Adam was very quiet last night," Helen said as Melanie got her settled into her chair after her exercises.

"Really?" Just the sound of Adam's name was enough to ignite a soft warmth deep within her. She had it even worse than Serena thought.

Helen slipped her glasses on and adjusted them lightly. "Didn't the two of you go to bring those letters to Donna?"

The two of you. As if they belonged together.

Love and helpless longing swept over her. Her head told her he was all wrong for her, but oh, her heart. It had its own rhythm, independent from her practical thoughts.

"Donna was very happy to get them. I'm really hoping and praying it will help get them together."

"Yes, it's sad to see someone alone who used to be a part of someone else." She sighed lightly. "I still miss my husband, and I know Adam misses Lana. Or at least being with someone." She turned to Melanie and caught her hand. "But I don't think he misses her as much as he used to."

Melanie couldn't stop the blush creeping up her neck, warming her cheeks. She felt as if the imprint of Adam's lips were visible on her lips. Her forehead, her temples.

"Well, once he moves to the city, I'm sure he'll find someone," she said quietly.

"Maybe." Helen stroked Melanie's hand. "You don't like the city, do you?" Helen's blue eyes, magnified behind her glasses, were fixed on Melanie, but Melanie sensed a deeper meaning behind the question.

"I could get a job in a hospital in the city, but I prefer living in the country."

"And you prefer someone who shares your faith." Helen's quiet statement held a tone of resignation.

Melanie just nodded, knowing exactly what Helen was asking her.

"Adam has been through a lot of pain since Lana died. And guilt." Helen clung to Melanie's hand, as if pleading with a judge for the life of her child. "He used to believe in God's love. You can show him the way back."

Her words echoed Melanie's own confusion. Last night as her thoughts twisted and spun, she had prayed, cried. Searched the Scriptures for strength and direction. She knew her feelings for Adam were stronger each time she saw him. And she also knew that each time they were together she tried to find a way to get around the principles and limitations she had placed on herself.

Melanie closed her eyes, praying for wisdom. For guidance.

"I can't be the one to do that," Melanie confided.

"I'm sorry if I stepped out of line, Melanie, but I know he cares for you, too." Helen let go of Melanie's hand. "Can't you help him?"

"Adam has to find the way on his own," Melanie said, holding Helen's longing gaze. "He has to commit his life to Christ separate from any emotions or feelings he might have for me."

Helen sighed lightly. "You're right, Melanie. You're a very wise girl. And I hope my son comes to his senses. Before it's too late."

Melanie could say nothing to that. Her own emotions were fragile where Adam was concerned.

"Are you going to say goodbye to Adam before you go?"

Melanie nodded, thinking of the papers she had slipped into her briefcase. In spite of, or maybe even because of, her personal feelings for him, Adam had to know what she had discovered. For his sake. Only his sake.

Melanie slipped the strap of her briefcase over her shoulder as she stepped out onto the back deck. She took a moment to look over the yard, appreciating how much neater it was since she had first seen it.

Adam had removed all the piles of lumber. The bricks. The lawn was mowed and the hedge along the back was trimmed. He'd even cleaned out the flower beds, and under Helen's direction had planted a few perrenials.

Melanie waited for the familiar flush of ownership to come over her. But this time a hue of melancholy colored it.

What was a single woman like her doing, buying a house this size?

No second thoughts, she reminded herself. The papers have been signed. The down payment was sitting in a trust account, waiting for the take-over date. This is what you wanted.

She opened the door of the shop and went inside. The tang of sawdust and shavings hung in the air. A promise of things fresh and new.

Adam was standing by his workbench, his back to Melanie. Tiffany squatted on the bench looking at what Adam was working on.

"So, punkin, what colour should we paint the outside?"

As Adam moved, Melanie could see what he was talking about. It was a dollhouse complete with tiny shutters at the windows, a little porch with a railing.

Melanie felt a surprising clench of jealousy. She had never had a dollhouse, though she had always yearned for one.

"I have pink paint, blue paint or green paint," Adam was saying.

Tiffany bit her lip, shifting her weight from one

foot to the other as she squinted at the little house. "I like pink."

Adam smiled at her. "Pink it is." He lifted her off the bench and gave her a quick hug before setting her down on the ground. As he looked up he saw Melanie.

Straightened.

His eyes lit briefly with a penetrating light that seemed to pierce her soul. Melanie wavered under the intensity of his gaze.

Then as briefly as it had come, the light vanished, he blinked and he was smiling a careful, welcoming smile.

"Well, hi there, Melanie."

Tiffany whirled around at the sound of her name. "Mellalie," she called out, launching herself at Melanie. "Daddy made me a house."

"I see that." Melanie caught the little girl and swung her around.

Tiffany pressed her warm palms against Melanie's cheeks, holding her gaze. "It's my own house, just for me. You come and see it." Tiffany wiggled in Melanie's arms. Melanie let her down and then followed her to the workbench.

"Up, Daddy." She held her arms up to Adam.

Adam frowned down at her. "Pardon me?"

"Up, please, Daddy," she amended with a coy smile.

Adam lifted her up and gave her a quick hug before he set her down on the bench again.

"She called you Daddy," Melanie said quietly, amazed as the realization struck her.

Adam flashed her a self-conscious smile. "Yeah. She just started last night."

Melanie held his gaze, smiling. "I'm happy for you. Looks like things are coming together."

"At least on the home front. I just wish Kyle would get off my back."

Trepidation shivered down Melanie's spine at the mention of Kyle. "If you need the money any sooner, I can give Bob a push," she said quickly, hoping she sounded more relaxed than she felt. As long as the loan was in abeyance, as long as the take-over date was in the nebulous future, she could fool herself into thinking that maybe things could change. "He says he's waiting for an employer's report."

"No need to rush. Kyle needs the money for some engineer reports on a spec project." Adam tucked a wisp of hair behind Tiffany's ear and let his hand linger on her cheek. "He can wait."

Don't read more into that than what he's saying, Melanie thought.

"Lovely little house," she said, stepping closer to the workbench, moving into safer territory.

"I had some time on my hands and thought I would use some of the scraps left over from the dresser. I got the idea from you, actually." Adam pulled the cuff of his shirtsleeve over his hand and wiped off some sawdust from the side.

"You're a lucky little girl, Tiffany." Melanie stroked the little girl's head, noticing that her hair was sprinkled with shavings and sawdust.

Tiffany lay on her stomach on the workbench, busy

opening and closing the front door of the house, happily ignoring both of them.

Adam leaned back against the workbench, his arms folded over his chest. A sense of expectation thrummed through the air as their gazes met.

"How's my mom doing?"

"Really well." Melanie fiddled with the strap of her briefcase, her eyes flicking away from his, then returning like a homing pigeon. "Her hip is healing much better than I expected, and I'm sure you could move her any day now."

"That's good to know."

The inane words and conversation were a thin veneer over deeper, stronger emotions. But where could they go beyond the impasse they had reached last night? Nothing had changed in the past fourteen hours, yet for Melanie it was as if everything was different. She knew she was in danger of falling in love with this man.

Adam cleared his throat, shifted his weight. "I, uh, was wondering if you're busy on Sunday."

Her heart jumped in her chest. What did he mean by this? What did he want?

"I'm not. Why do you ask?"

"I got a phone call from Sandy Gerrard today. She invited me to her parents' anniversary party on Sunday." He pulled his lower lip between his teeth as he studied her.

Melanie breathed in long and slowly. "I wouldn't belong there."

Adam pushed some sawdust into a pile with the toe

of his boot, then looked up at her, his blue eyes almost piercing.

Melanie was losing herself in his eyes even as he pushed himself away from the workbench. One step and he was in front of her. One movement and his fingers traced the line of her chin. "Please come with me, Melanie," he whispered. "I can't see Lana's parents on my own. It was your idea I see them, so I was hoping you could come with me."

She needed to take only one small step and she was in his arms. One movement and she sensed he would hold her close. She wanted to be held again. Wanted to feel supported and surrounded by strength and warmth.

Instead she took a step back. "Though I'm glad you're taking my advice, I don't think I should go. And I don't think you need my support."

Adam leaned back, his hands clasped around his neck. "You don't think so?" His voice held a tight edge she hadn't heard in a while. "I have only seen Lana's parents a couple of times since Lana died. And each time I've had to face parents who have lost a beloved daughter." Adam stopped. Dropped his head back and blew out a sigh. "It's hard, Melanie."

Melanie clutched the strap of her briefcase even harder, the edges cutting into her hands. "Is it because you feel guilty?"

Adam dragged his hands over his face. "Hard not to when each time I see Lana's mother, Amanda, she starts crying." Adam laughed, a sharp, bitter sound. "I can deal with contractors yelling at me, unwilling employees, demanding bank managers, but a woman's tears unman me. And Amanda's tears always bring back the guilt. Always.''

Melanie thought of the papers in her briefcase. "Can I talk to you outside? Do you have time?"

He nodded and Melanie followed Adam and Tiffany out of the shop.

What she had to tell him she wanted to deliver in warmth and sunshine. She hoped it would help him make a decision about going to the Gerrards.

More than that, she hoped it would break down the barriers between him and God.

Chapter Twelve

"Adam, how much did you know about Lana's diabetes?" Melanie asked as soon as they were seated in some lawn chairs beside the sandbox. Tiffany was already busy pouring sand into a pail, singing snatches of a song.

"Quite a bit. I had to in order to help her stay balanced. Why do you ask?"

"What did she ever tell you about her condition? Especially when she was pregnant?"

Adam crossed his arms over his chest, his posture defensive. "Melanie, why are you going into this? What old history are you trying to bring up?"

She had done this completely wrong. She was coming across like a nurse when Adam needed a friend.

She put the papers down and held his steady gaze. *Please Lord,* she prayed, *give me the right words. Help him to understand.* She knew she was going to be talking about someone he loved and she wanted to be fair.

"I had a conversation with an old doctor of Lana's. He made a comment I couldn't let go of. About how Lana resented her diabetes." Melanie fingered the papers, her eyes on his. "I think Lana's death had less to do with where you lived and more to do with how she managed her diabetes before she went into labor."

"What do you mean?" Adam's voice held a definite chill.

Tread carefully. Be diplomatic.

"I understand that Lana went to another doctor when she got pregnant."

Adam nodded. "Some doctor in Eastbar. She would phone here quite regularly."

"Did you know that Lana had missed a number of appointments the last three weeks before she went into labor?"

Adam frowned. Shook his head. "She went to Eastbar twice a week to see the doctor. Sandy always brought her or she'd go herself."

"She didn't go to the doctor, Adam. Nor did she do the daily blood tests she was supposed to be doing."

"How do you know about the blood tests? I saw her daily diary. Her sugars were always good."

Melanie heard the bafflement in his voice, saw the confusion in his eyes.

"I know I'm only supposing that she didn't do her tests," she said quietly. "But Sandy said she found a whole box of blood-testing strips that hadn't been touched. She didn't think anything of it until I phoned to ask her a few questions. Sandy and I both now think Lana fudged the diary just to keep things quiet. Sandy always wondered why her tests were always so good when she'd been hard to control before. If she'd gone to the doctor, she would have been able to prove or disprove Lana's test results with a Hemoglobin A, which is probably why she didn't go.''

''Why would Lana want to do that?''

''I don't know.'' Melanie riffled the papers, uneasy with what she was telling him. Yet she knew she had to continue. ''Had she taken care of herself, had she seen the doctor, she might still be alive.''

Adam melted back into his chair, his expression one of injured bafflement. ''Why did I not know? How could I not see?''

''You couldn't see because she wouldn't let you see.'' Melanie had to bite back the angry flow of words. Now, facing Adam's puzzled sadness, she felt anew the deceit Lana had been practicing. The chance she had been taking with Tiffany's health and well-being.

Adam shook his head, as if rearranging the new thoughts Melanie had placed there. ''So it had nothing to do with living here, or anywhere else for that matter?''

''I'm afraid not.'' Melanie couldn't stand the isolation of his pain. She reached out, caught his hand. He grasped it between both his, pressing it against his chest.

''Why did you do all this, Melanie?'' His voice was hoarse with emotion. ''Why did you think I needed to know this?''

Melanie curled her fingers around his, rubbing her

thumb over the back of his hand, his skin rough beneath her fingers. The hands of a working man. "I wanted you to go to the Gerrards knowing that it wasn't your fault. That whatever pain the Gerrards may feel was inflicted on them by their own daughter. Not by something you feel you should have done."

Adam clutched her hand against his chest, his eyes like a laser on hers.

"Yesterday I asked you why this matters so much to you and you said because you care." His chest rose beneath her hand in a sigh. "Today you're helping me lay my past to rest. Is it still because you care?"

Melanie held his gaze, unaware that she was drifting toward him until the armrest of the chair dug in to her side. She couldn't lie.

"Yes, I care, Adam. I care about you. I care about the guilt you can't let go of."

"Then don't give up on me yet, Melanie," he whispered. "Give me some time."

And then what? Go with him to the city? Try to convince him to stay here?

But she pushed the questions aside. Prayed that God would give her wisdom and guidance. Because she knew that she wanted to be with him in spite of everything she knew.

Adam lifted her hand to his mouth and pressed his lips on the inside of her palm.

"You've given me much to think about, Melanie," he said quietly. "I just need to sort a few things out."

She nodded, but gently pulled her hand back. She had her own questions and worries, but for today, for now, she was willing to leave them alone.

* * *

Adam closed the door to Tiffany's bedroom. It had taken a couple of stories, a drink and a little talk about Melanie, but Tiffany was finally asleep. He leaned back against the door, his mind a whirling welter of confused thoughts. It was as if the past three years had been uprooted and rearranged and he didn't know where to put his memories anymore.

The guilt he had been carrying had not been his to bear.

Just as Melanie had said from the first.

But why had Lana potentially endangered their child's health? Why, in the last vital weeks of her pregnancy, had she not taken better care of herself?

As his thoughts spun and twisted, old memories surfaced. Lana, shaky from yet another insulin reaction. Him finding chocolate bar wrappers hidden under the seat of the car, under the couch. Like a little girl, she would sneak food that she shouldn't have been eating.

Lana had made some bad choices, and he might never know the reasons.

But in spite of the memories and the questions, he felt as if a huge weight had been lifted off his shoulders. What Melanie had told him gently removed the bitter sting of regret, of wishing he could relive those last moments. He couldn't have prevented what happened. Postponed it, maybe.

The thought, though it comforted, also saddened him. He had given Lana everything she wanted. She'd had so much more than many people. Why wasn't she happier?

He pushed himself away from the wall, and walked slowly down the stairs.

The door to his mother's room was still open, the soft light beckoning. He knocked lightly and opened the door farther.

Helen looked up from the book she was reading and laid it carefully on the bed in front of her.

"Hey, Mom, you can't sleep?" he asked, stepping into the room.

"I'm just doing my evening devotions."

"Mind if I sit with you awhile?" He sat in the chair in the corner of the room and looked around. The soft light enhanced the pale yellow of the walls, creating a gentle haven.

"You look tired, Adam."

"Busy day. Lots to think about."

"Melanie seemed a little distracted, as well. I asked her about her visit with Donna. She was so happy you took her. She said it was like an answer to prayer. How wonderful that God could have used you like that."

There it was again. God in control of his life. "Can God use someone who hasn't talked to Him? Someone who has turned his back on Him?" Where once his words might have held bitterness, now, after what Melanie had told him, they held sorrow. Regret.

"God is always seeking you, Adam." Helen's voice grew quiet while she ran her fingers along the edge of her Bible. "He hasn't turned His back on you, in spite of your bitterness over Lana's death."

Lana.

Adam looked around the room he and Lana had

worked so hard on. Thought of the dreams they had spun when they found out she was expecting a baby. This house was going to be more than a dream—it was going to be a home for them and their child.

And she had thrown it all away.

He sighed lightly and laid his head on the back of the chair. He felt unaccountably weary. As if he'd been running for miles. Aimless miles.

"Do you want me to read to you, Adam?" Helen asked, her voice a soft sound.

It had been three years since Adam had opened a Bible for himself. When his mother would come to visit, she would read to him. He'd just never listened.

But now?

"Sure, Mom. Go ahead."

"This is from Psalm 51." She cleared her throat, adjusted her glasses as she always did. Her own small preparation for speaking aloud the words of God.

And this time he listened. Tried to draw the words into his emptiness.

"'Have mercy on me, O God, according to Your unfailing love; according to Your great compassion blot out my transgressions.'" His mother's quiet, reverent voice touched old memories, drew up old emotions.

"'Against You and You only have I sinned.'"

The words shook Adam. He had not done wrong by Lana. If he had done wrong, it was to blame God for Lana's death. His sin was against God alone.

"'Restore to me the joy of Your salvation and grant me a willing spirit, to sustain me.'"

How long had it been since he had felt joy? Since

he could truly say he was happy? Had he been caught up in the guilt phase of grieving, as Donna had said she had been? Had he wrongly blamed God when it was his own sorrow he hadn't dealt with that was holding him back?

He'd thought he could live without God, but the emptiness in his life attested to the fact that he couldn't. But how to come back? God was all-powerful and not to be trifled with.

"'The sacrifices of God are a broken spirit; a broken and contrite heart, O God, You will not despise.'"

"Is that all it takes, Mom?" Adam asked, lifting his head to look at his mother. "It sounds too easy."

Helen smiled. "It's a beginning, Adam. The beginning of dying to self and living to Christ. You've heard this all your life."

"I know I have. But lately my life has been so far from redemption, I don't know where to start."

"How about praying with me now? And on Sunday, well, there's always church."

"So, girlie. Here we are." Adam set Tiffany down on the pavement of the parking lot and fluffed out her dress. He wiped a smudge of jam from the corner of her mouth and smiled at her. "Are you ready for church, sweetie?"

She nodded exuberantly, her pigtails bobbing up and down. His mother had taken the time to do Tiffany's hair, but had decided to stay home from church this morning. Said she wasn't feeling well, though to him she looked fine.

Adam had wanted her with him when he faced the inside of the church once again.

The last time he'd been in the building was Lana's funeral.

"Restore to me the joy of Your salvation." The words his mother had read last night slipped into his mind. Smoothed the residue of guilt.

"Daddy, Daddy, I see Mellalie."

Funny how the mere mention of her name flipped his heart. He looked in the direction Tiffany was pointing and saw her. She was wearing a dress again, simple yet elegant. It set off her hair. Hair that caught the sun and sent out auburn rays as she stopped and turned toward them.

As their eyes met, Adam felt his breathing slow. Once again he was aware of the sensation of time falling away. He saw her lips move, mouth his name.

Still holding his hand, Tiffany leaned away from him. "Come, Daddy," she demanded. "Let's go see Mellalie."

Adam didn't resist Tiffany's leading, following her easily to Melanie's side.

"Hello, Adam," Melanie said, her voice soft, almost breathless. "So glad you could come."

Adam thought she might say more, might make a comment, but thankfully all she did was crouch in front of Tiffany, unhampered by the narrow cut of her dress. "Hey, sweetie. You look pretty today."

"Gramma did my hair."

Melanie looked up at Adam. "Where is your mother today?"

"She says she's not feeling well."

"Is she spiking a temp?" Melanie got up, frowning as she adjusted her purse on her shoulder.

"I checked, but she seemed fine. Maybe just tired. She said she would catch a service on one of the radio stations."

"And you didn't want to stay home with her?" Though Melanie's oblique question was softly spoken, Adam clearly heard the meaning behind it.

"No. I thought I would come to church today."

"And why was that?"

Adam held her eyes, questions still hovering. "I'm not entirely sure myself."

Her full rich smile sent his heart pounding against his chest. "Well, I'm glad you're here."

He was glad, too. After her revelation and his talk with his mother, Adam needed more than ever the comfort he might find in church and with Melanie.

Tiffany took Melanie's hand as a matter of course and started pulling them toward the church building.

"She's eager to go," Melanie said with a light laugh. "Has she been before?"

Adam shook his head with a rueful glance Melanie's way. "I have never taken her."

The usher at the back of the church greeted Melanie warmly, holding her hand a little longer than was necessary, Adam thought.

An awkward moment followed as they stood in the entrance to the sanctuary. Adam didn't know if he should ask Melanie to sit with them. She had given him no indication of how she felt about what he had asked her the other day.

Thankfully Tiffany resolved the dilemma.

"You sit with us," Tiffany said, tugging on Melanie's hand.

Melanie glanced at Adam and smiled. "I guess that settles that."

Adam smiled back. "Don't mess with a three-year-old."

As they settled in the pew he could see women sidling closer, heads bent, heard whispers swelling.

He knew how it looked. Melanie had obviously been attending church for a while and suddenly one Sunday she shows up with the prodigal son and his daughter.

Like a little family.

He ignored the whispers as he settled Tiffany in between them, avoiding Melanie's gaze, pretending to be engrossed in the bulletin of events. After a few minutes he looked up at the front of the church.

The flood of memories assaulted his equilibrium. Lana's casket buried under a mound of flowers. A picture of Lana perched on top. He clenched the bulletin, fighting the surprising wave of sorrow. It didn't have to happen, he thought.

But this time the guilt that normally accompanied thoughts of Lana's needless death was assuaged by what Melanie had told him.

Lana had made her own decisions, and he and Tiffany had paid the price for that.

"Are you okay?"

Melanie's light touch on his forearm, her voice laced with concern broke through the swirling emotions.

Without stopping to analyze, he clamped his hand

down on hers, his gaze locked on hers, like a storm-tossed ship catching the saving beacon from a lighthouse.

"Is something wrong?" she repeated, leaning a little closer.

He held her amber eyes, unable to look away. "I'm okay," he returned softly, his hand still pressed against hers, her skin soft and warm beneath his. He moved his thumb back and forth over the back of her hand as a gentle peace suffused his soul.

Tiffany slapped her hand on top of Adam's, breaking the moment. "Your turn, Mellalie," she said, nudging Melanie with her elbow.

Melanie blinked, then turned to Tiffany. "Okay," she whispered, laying her hand on top of Tiffany's.

"You can't go, Daddy, so I hafta."

Tiffany laid her hand on top of the stack. It was their little game they'd starting playing at night when he tucked her in. Having Melanie's hands mingled in with his and Tiffany's was true and good.

And where was it going? He had asked her for time to sort out his nebulous feelings. But each time he saw her he knew he cared more.

He pulled his hand back, eliciting a disappointed cry from his daughter.

"Shh, Tiffany. We're in church," he said, bending over her, not daring to look at Melanie.

He knew he had his own obligations. A business that needed him. A mother. A daughter.

Yet each time he was with her, his feelings for her changed. Grew. He had asked her for time and he knew he had to give himself that space, as well. So much had changed in the past two days. He needed to absorb it. Realign his relationship with God.

As people filled up the benches in front of them and beside them, he focused his attention on them. He recognized many of the people, though the names eluded him. Some greeted him by name. Some stopped to chat. Most said something to Melanie, as well.

Thankfully Tiffany sat quietly between him and Melanie, content to scribble with a pencil Melanie had given her on the children's bulletin Melanie had taken.

Adam looked again at the front of the church, this time deliberately remembering the day of the funeral. In spite of what Melanie had told him, he couldn't completely eradicate the emotions that had been a part of his life for almost three years. In unguarded moments he could still feel the hollow clench of regret.

"Against You and You only have I sinned."

The words his mother had read to him braided themselves through his thoughts.

He had come to church this morning on the advice of his mother. And, if he were honest with himself, because he'd hoped to see Melanie.

Was he being fair to her? She wanted a Christian man. Someone who was willing to stay in this small town.

Could he stay here?

The thought wove through his other thoughts, twisting and pulling.

Finally the minister strode to the front of the

church, and with a booming voice announced the first song.

The congregation rose to its feet as an overhead screen descended from one corner at the front.

This was new. So was the song. Melanie knew it and sang along.

Her voice carried, clear and true and ringing with conviction. He couldn't keep his eyes off her. A peaceful smile curved her lips, and as she sang, he saw deep love and a strong faith.

He envied her.

The minister wended his way through the liturgy, and when the time came for the children to leave for Children's Church, Tiffany was a deadweight against his side. She was fast asleep. Adam glanced at Melanie, remembering her offer to take Tiffany out, but she noticed, too.

She gave him a careful smile, aware of his withdrawal, then looked ahead.

The minister announced the text of the sermon.

Psalm 51.

A chill shivered up his spine as for the second time he heard God's call to him. The reminder of whom Adam had sinned against.

Not Lana. Not her family. His anger and rebellion had been directed at God.

He drew his sleeping daughter close, as if bracing for an assault.

As the minister preached, his words were a reminder of the call God extends again and again. Of God's sacrificial love.

Adam listened, like a man who had been thirsty so

long, he had forgotten what water could do. The message filtered through his confusion, rearranged thoughts that had already been tossed about by what he had learned from Melanie.

"It's not our strength that brings us to God, but the strength of His love. His forgiveness that draws us to Him," the minister said, his voice ringing with conviction. "It is sheer grace. All of our sins from greatest to smallest are an issue with God. And who better to deal with them but a merciful, just and loving Father who wants us back."

"Against You and You only have I sinned…. A broken and contrite heart, O God, You will not despise."

Adam felt all the resistance he had put up against God, all the walls and barriers he had erected in his anger and guilt, slowly melt away, washed like the sand on the beach beneath the slow relentless waves.

He had been adrift. Lost. Striking out at God. But God still called him back in spite of what he had done.

It seemed too easy. It seemed too wonderful.

The organist and pianist struck up the opening chords of the next song just as Adam turned to it one-handed.

"When Peace like a River."

Adam clenched the spine of the book as the words pounded against him just like the sea billows in the song.

They had sung this song at Lana's funeral.

He closed his eyes, clinging to his daughter, as his throat thickened.

And the first tears he had shed since Lana's funeral squeezed from between his eyelids.

Forgive me, Father, he prayed. *Forgive me my anger, my sin, my involvement in myself. Let it be well with my soul.*

Chapter Thirteen

Melanie sang the words of the song by rote, her eyes on the book in front of her but her entire attention focused on Adam sitting beside her.

What in the song had prompted this public unveiling? Had what she told him the other day brought out new grief?

She glanced at him again, then away as he wiped a track of moisture from his cheek. She'd seen sorrow manifested in many forms, yet the sight of Adam, his head bent over his sleeping daughter as tears slid down his cheeks, created an echoing pain.

He looked so alone. She didn't stop to think how anyone around her might see her actions, responding instead to his silent need.

She slipped her arm along his broad back, her hand cupping his far shoulder. He shifted ever so slightly toward her as if drawing from her strength.

The final triumphant words of the song resounded

through the building "It is well, it is well with my soul."

She felt Adam draw a shuddering breath, then another, and his head slowly came up. Once again his hand caught hers.

He didn't need to look at her. It was as if they had connected on another level, moved to another part of their relationship.

Then she felt his shoulders straighten, as if his strength had returned. She lowered her arm and drew her hand back.

The last notes of the doxology echoed and faded away, then after a moment of silence the first quiet notes of the postlude drifted down through the sanctuary.

As if suddenly released, voices rose in conversation, papers were shuffled and energy flowed through the building as people moved toward the exits.

Melanie, suddenly conscious of how close she sat to Adam, gently pulled away. An older couple in front of them turned around and greeted Adam, smiled at Tiffany, who still slept.

Melanie felt suddenly out of place and got to her feet. Adam stayed sitting, chatting with the couple. He glanced her way, as if he wanted to say something, but the woman asked him a question and he looked back at her.

"Melanie, how are you?"

The woman behind her tapped Melanie on the shoulder. Freda Hartshorn, another nurse from the health unit.

"Have you heard anything about your job?"

"Not yet," Melanie said, turning reluctantly to Freda. "I'm seeing the supervisor Monday."

"She's a different sort, but I wouldn't worry about it." Freda's eyes slipped away as she spoke, and Melanie knew exactly where she was looking. And she knew exactly what Freda's next topic might be.

"By the way, how's Mrs. Wierenga doing?" Melanie asked, hoping to sidetrack her.

Freda dragged her reluctant gaze back to Melanie.

"She's okay." Freda began walking out of the pew and Melanie followed, hopefully forestalling any questions Freda might have about Adam.

Melanie made the usual small talk, even though she wanted nothing more than to stay with Adam. To somehow offer him what comfort she could give him.

But that would have given people even more things to talk about, more questions to ask. What had just happened had created a subtle shift in their relationship, a movement to an unknown destination pushed along by Adam's ambiguous question the other day. She needed a little bit of distance. Some time to think.

By the time she and Freda had made it out the back door, she finally chanced a look behind her.

Adam and Tiffany were nowhere to be seen.

She made small talk with a few other people, turned down an offer to come for lunch and rescheduled an appointment she had with an older man this week, all the while keeping a friendly smile on her face.

Beneath that, however, her emotions twisted and spun.

A couple of days ago she was in Adam's arms. He had kissed her. And today he had come to church.

She finished up the conversation she was having with a friendly young teenager who wanted her to help with the youth group.

Then, just as she turned to leave, she saw him. He was working his way toward her through the thinning group of people.

"I'm sorry about that," he said when he finally made it to her side. "I got waylaid by some old friends. Then I looked up and you were gone."

He shifted his still-sleeping daughter in his arms. His smile was careful, almost hesitant, as if bruised by the emotions of the service. "Do you want to go for coffee?"

Funny how that cautiously worded invitation sent her heart soaring.

"I'd like that very much," she said, returning his smile. "What about Tiffany?"

Adam pulled his chin back as if taking another look at his little girl. "Once she wakes up she might be a bit cranky, but if you're around, I'm sure she'll be fine. She seems to have formed quite an attachment to you."

Melanie couldn't stop herself from reaching out and touching Tiffany lightly on one rosy cheek. "The feeling is mutual," Melanie said softly.

In her peripheral vision Melanie saw a movement. A woman stopped beside them. Laid her hand on Adam's arm as she greeted him. It was Sandy Gerrard.

She wore a loose flowing dress today, her shining

blond hair tumbling over her shoulders. She turned to Melanie, her attitude reserved. "Hi, Melanie. How are you?"

"I'm good, thanks." Melanie kept her voice casual, but she could sense Sandy's restraint. Melanie suspected it had much to do with the phone call they had shared a few days ago. It must have been hard to relive what had happened three years ago. To raise suspicions over why her sister had died.

So Melanie said nothing more. Not that it mattered.

Sandy's attention was focused intently on Adam, her hand resting on his forearm. "It's so good to see you here, Adam. I usually go to church in Eastbar with Mom and Dad, but I'm visiting a friend. I'm glad I ran into you. Now I can remind you of Mom and Dad's anniversary picnic today."

Adam just nodded his acknowledgment.

"Please come," Sandy pleaded, leaning closer to him. "It's been so long since Mom and Dad saw you. Since we all saw you." Her voice lowered on the last words, and her eyes rose to his.

She's in love with him, Melanie thought with a jolt.

"Your mother is welcome, too," Sandy added quickly. "Is she here today?"

"No. She's not feeling well. And I had other plans." Adam glanced over at Melanie. Was it her own foolish hopefulness or did she read entreaty in his eyes?

Tiffany squirmed in Adam's arms, stretched out and whimpered. She blinked, caught sight of Melanie and reached out to her.

Once again Melanie automatically responded by taking the bundle of warm little girl into her arms.

Too late she saw Sandy's pained expression. "I'm sorry. I didn't think…" Melanie stumbled over her words. "Did you want to hold her?" She tried to hand Tiffany to Sandy.

But Tiffany clung to Melanie, burying her head in Melanie's neck as her damp fingers twisted in Melanie's hair.

"She's always like this when she just wakes up," Melanie said with an apologetic smile. Again Melanie realized how that sounded. As if she, a stranger to the Gerrard family, knew more about the daily habits of their niece and granddaughter than Sandy did.

Trouble was, she probably did.

"You're welcome to come, too, Melanie," Sandy said. She gently touched Tiffany's cheek, then turned back to Adam as if dismissing Melanie. "It's been so long since you've talked to Mom and Dad. I know they'd love to see you."

Adam glanced back at Melanie. "Your parents have quite a few advocates, it seems."

Sandy's smile blossomed. "Then we'll see you there?"

"I suppose." Adam breathed out his acceptance on a sigh, gave Sandy a vague smile and watched her go.

Melanie waited until Sandy was out of earshot. "I don't know if it's such a good idea that I come along," she said, absently stroking Tiffany's head with her chin. "I think it might be best if you spend the time with Lana's family on your own."

Adam turned to Melanie again, his smile gentle. "I don't want to be alone with Lana's family. And I'd like you to come."

She was lost, Melanie realized, drifting into the gentle snare of his eyes. How could she withstand the potency of those incredibly blue eyes, the gentle smile playing over his lips?

Be careful.

The warning wended its slow, torturous way to the front of her mind. Nothing was definite between them.

But today she didn't want to go back to her lonely apartment. She didn't want to spend Sunday afternoon by herself. Again. She wanted to be with Adam. She wanted Tiffany in her arms.

"Okay," she said, pressing her cheek to Tiffany's warm, damp curls. "I'll come. But I'll take my own car."

"No problem. But I'd like you to come with me to pick up Mom. She'll probably come along if she knows you're coming, too."

"I'll see you at the house, then." She carefully handed Tiffany over to her father. Thankfully she went without a murmur.

As Melanie got into her car, she pushed a cassette tape into the deck. The music immediately filled the car, pushing out second thoughts and concerns. Adam had asked for time.

Well, that was exactly what she was giving him.

The Gerrards lived almost half an hour away from Derwin and Melanie was thankful she was following Adam. After a number of confusing twists and turns, the taillights of Adam's truck flashed as he signaled to make a turn into a driveway.

As they pulled up to the house, Melanie's second thoughts clamored for attention.

In the center of the yard stood a white canopy, decorated with streamers and flowers. Older people sat on chairs in the shade of the large poplar trees, younger people hung around the vehicles parked row upon row outside the fenced-in yard. Little children ran around screaming and calling out names of other children. Women scurried between the house and the tent carrying plates and casserole dishes and bowls.

This wasn't the cozy family get-together that Sandy had implied. It was a full-fledged party.

"The Gerrards are quite a bunch, aren't they?" Helen said as Adam helped her out of the truck. When Melanie had stopped by the Engler place, she had half hoped Helen was still not feeling well and would want to stay home. But Helen, looking surprisingly well, had pronounced herself rested and eager to get out, which had made Melanie wonder how "ill" Helen had been that morning.

"Are they all family?" Melanie asked.

Helen sniffed and pursed her lips as she assessed the gathering. "Pretty much," she announced.

"It can be rather overwhelming when you first see them all together like this," Adam said, setting Tiffany on the ground. He tugged the cuffs of his shirt down and ran his fingers through his hair, his eyes on the yard. Pulled in a deep breath.

"You look fine, son." Helen tweaked his collar into place, then patted him on the chest.

"Just watch this step now, Helen," Melanie said as Adam guided her and her walker through the gate. They found an empty chair and settled Helen in.

"Can I get you anything?" Adam asked.

"I'm fine. See, here's an old friend come to say hello."

"Helen, my dear, you certainly don't look like you've just had surgery." An elderly man stopped beside them, his pale gray suit almost the same shade as his thinning hair. He took Helen's hand between his, smiling down on her, his clipped mustache bobbing upward. "Helen, you are as beautiful as you ever were."

A faint flush colored Helen's cheeks as she coyly ducked her head.

She was flirting with him, Melanie thought, trying not to smile.

"Adam, Melanie, this is Mr. Edgar Matheson. Edgar, this is my long-lost son." Helen waved a hand at Adam and then nodded at Melanie. "And this is my health nurse and good friend, Melanie Visser."

Mr. Matheson's gray eyes fixed on Melanie. "You look very familiar."

Memories of her earlier time in Derwin slipped easily back. This very dapper gentleman hadn't changed much since junior high school. "You were my chemistry teacher."

"Ah, yes." Edgar Matheson inclined his head, his eyes crinkling at the corners as he smiled. "How could I forget those unique amber eyes? I remember how a girl named Roxanne used to tease you in class."

''That was a long time ago.'' Melanie dismissed his comment with a light shrug. ''It hasn't created any lasting effects.'' Nothing like Adam's casual rescue of her after one particularly bad bout of teasing.

''Well, you've certainly turned into a lovely young woman.''

''And you, Edgar, are the same unrepentant flirt you ever were.'' Helen turned to Melanie. ''Why don't you give me that little girl? And the two of you can go say hello to the Gerrards. Tell them that I have Tiffany. Edgar and I have a lot to catch up on.'' Helen held Melanie's gaze with a rock-hard steadiness that Melanie knew she couldn't shake. If she resisted, Helen would resist back and create an awkward situation in front of an old teacher.

They settled Tiffany on a chair beside Helen. Thankfully she seemed content to sit and page through the books Adam had had the foresight to bring along from home.

When they were out of earshot of Helen, Melanie stopped, about to explain to Adam why he should go alone, when he caught Melanie's arm, pulling her gently aside. A boisterous group of children screamed past them. When they were gone, he didn't let go of her, though, his thumb gently stroking her forearm.

''Do you remember that time I found Roxanne teasing you?'' he asked, his expression bemused. ''I had forgotten about it until now.''

Gentle shivers chased themselves up and down her arm, instigated by his touch, and his eyes delved into hers, as if probing her deepest secrets.

''You held out your hand to me,'' Melanie said

softly, unable to look away from the mesmerizing blue of his eyes. "You said, 'I've been waiting for you.' And then we walked away together. You rescued me."

"And you've rescued me." Adam's smile faded away, and his hand stilled on her arm. Tightened. "This morning in church I felt the sadness I had when Lana died, but this time without the crushing, twisting guilt." He angled his head to one side, studying her face. "I want to thank you for that. I wish I knew exactly where to go from here...."

"You don't need to have all the answers right now, Adam," Melanie said, determined not to let her own loneliness cloud the issues he had to work through. Just because he had come to church didn't mean he was ready for God yet. "You have some things to deal with that will help you decide. Let God work how He will in your life."

"You have such a strong faith," Adam said softly, touching her cheek lightly. His fingers cupped her chin. "I envy that."

As if it moved on its own, her hand rose. Pressed against his as her eyes drifted shut.

Just a moment, she promised herself.

Then she lowered her hand. Looked away.

"I have my own struggles," she said quietly.

Struggles with a confused man I'm finding far too appealing. And a little girl I long to care for as my own. And a house that is growing too important in my life. She stepped back, determined to give them both the distance they needed. "Now you better go and find the Gerrards or they are going to wonder if you ever made it here.''

Adam caught her hand. ''That sounds like you might not come with me.''

Melanie hesitated. She knew she was there only on sufferance. She shouldn't have come. Adam hadn't seen the Gerrards since he had arrived and it wouldn't look good if he showed up with an unknown woman at his side.

''Please come with me.'' He squeezed her hands. ''I don't know if I can do this by myself.''

How could she say no? Adam was always so strong. So confident. Now he was almost pleading for her to come with him.

And she was foolish enough to catch on to that and allow him to lead her on.

It wasn't difficult to find Amanda and Tom Gerrard. They stood in the center of a group of well-wishers. Amanda wore a spray of flowers pinned to the jacket of a pale yellow suit. Tom stood beside her, his arm over her shoulders. They were laughing, the picture of joy and celebration.

Envy tugged at Melanie for their happiness with each other and the longevity of their relationship. It was what she wanted more than anything else. To be able to celebrate a thirty-year anniversary with friends and family.

Then Tom turned.

Melanie saw his eyes flicker from Adam to her and his smile disappeared. He nudged his wife, whose face went through the same transformation.

''Adam,'' Tom said with forced heartiness. ''So

glad you could come." He held out his hand to his son-in-law even as his eyes assessed Melanie.

Melanie held back while Amanda also greeted Adam with a smile. Also gave Melanie a less-than-welcoming glance.

Melanie understood then what was happening. Adam had been married to their daughter and it must have been hard for them to see him with someone else. Even though there was nothing more than dreams and wishes that kept her at Adam's side.

Amanda gave Adam a perfunctory hug and then looked away. Melanie could see tears in her eyes.

Adam turned to Melanie and drew her forward. "Tom and Amanda, I'd like you to meet Melanie. She's my mother's health nurse."

"Congratulations on your anniversary," Melanie said, holding out her hand. Tom's handshake was brief. Amanda merely nodded at her.

The other people surrounding them slowly drifted away, leaving the four of them alone.

"I'd like to echo Melanie's congratulations. And wishes for many more," Adam said, slipping his hands into his pockets.

An awkward silence followed his comments. Tom rocked back and forth, looking down at the ground. Amanda chewed her lower lip.

"We met Sandy after church," Adam continued. "She invited both of us to come."

"I see." Amanda glanced quickly from Adam to Melanie as if assessing their relationship. "So you're Helen's nurse. That was nice of you to take time to come with her. You don't need to be with her now?"

"Oh, no. She's doing quite well. Adam and I left her chatting with an old friend."

Amanda's sharp intake of breath told Melanie more than words could what Amanda thought of Melanie's casual linking of their names.

"I see," Amanda said softly, her hard gaze flicking from Adam to Melanie.

"I hear from Graydon that the carpentry business is going quite well," Adam said to Tom, seemingly oblivious to the tension that gripped Amanda.

"Absolutely. Absolutely." Tom grabbed the conversational hook like a drowning man. "We've got more work than we can handle. Graydon is looking at adding on to the shop and upgrading some of the woodworking tools."

While Adam and Tom chatted, Melanie kept her eyes fixed on them, wondering how long she dared stay here, the blatant object of Amanda's displeasure and discomfort.

"Where's Tiffany?" Amanda finally asked Adam during a lull in the conversation.

"Melanie and I left her with my mom."

Melanie almost cringed at Adam's words, echoing her own previously. Amanda's gaze glanced off Melanie, clung to Adam. "We haven't seen as much of her as we would have liked to," she said with a wounded tone.

"You've seen her a number of times already. And you know where we live in Calgary." Adam kept his voice even, but Melanie could sense his withdrawal.

"It's such a long way away," Amanda said, twisting her hands around each other. "You know how I hate driving. Just like Lana did."

"Amanda, be careful," Tom murmured. "Adam doesn't want to talk about Lana."

"She was our daughter. We loved her. Adam seems content to forget her." Amanda's gaze fell pointedly on Melanie.

Melanie felt the bolt of Amanda's anger. She didn't want to look away, but didn't know how to deal with such blatant animosity and still be polite.

And once again Adam came to her rescue. He moved a step closer to Melanie. Put his arm around her and drew her to his side.

"Lana died three years ago, Amanda. I loved her, too, and I haven't forgotten her, but I know when it's time to move on."

Amanda sniffed and wiped her eyes.

Before she could speak, however, Sandy was at Adam's side.

"Adam, you did come. I'm so glad." Sandy slipped her arm into Adam's other one and pulled him close. "How are you doing?"

"Not bad." His clipped voice gave lie to the words. Melanie ached for him even as she could feel herself slowly being pushed aside.

"I saw your mother and started looking for you. Tiffany is still with her, in case you were wondering." Sandy turned to her parents. "Isn't it lovely that Adam is here?"

"Of course it is," Amanda said with false heartiness.

"Did you have a chance to see what Mom and Dad

did to the kitchen?'' Sandy asked. ''Mom finally got rid of that pink countertop she's hated all these years.''

''My feelings weren't that strong.'' Amanda waved the comment away. But she was smiling now. Sandy's presence had eased the palpable tension.

''I don't know about that,'' Sandy said with a grin. ''Remember how she used to put hot frying pans directly on the counter, hoping she would scorch it?''

Adam didn't reply, but Melanie saw his mouth twitch with amusement at the memory.

Sandy smiled up at him, her gaze affectionate. ''I'm so glad you came back,'' she murmured. ''We've missed you.''

''But I hear you're selling Lana's house?'' Amanda demanded. ''That can't be right.''

Melanie's prick of resentment was followed by pity for Adam and a new understanding of the role Lana's parents had played in the burden of guilt Adam had carried.

''Melanie is buying it,'' Adam said.

Melanie's heart did a quick dive at the practical tone of his voice. The juxtaposition of Adam's arm around her while he spoke so casually of her buying the house so he could move on created a flurry of emotions that she couldn't identify.

Where were she and Adam headed? Anywhere?

Amanda's frown told Melanie exactly what she thought of Melanie moving into her daughter's former house. ''Why would a single girl like you want to buy that house?''

Melanie stifled her annoyance, reminding herself

that though Lana had died three years ago, Amanda, too, had her own sorrow to deal with. "It's a lovely place," she said, determined not to let Amanda's disapproval usurp even the smallest scrap of pleasure she got from the thought of owning that house. Determined not to read too much into the warmth of Adam's arm. She pulled away from him, giving herself distance from him and the emotions he raised in her. "It's going to be a home for me, as well as a good investment."

The practical comment injected a more businesslike tone to a very emotional conversation.

Still, Amanda's breath puffed out in displeasure.

And beside her she could feel Adam's confusion at her retreat.

"I remember how excited Lana was when she first found that house," Sandy said, pulling Adam closer to her.

As if on cue, Tom and Amanda moved closer to Sandy and Adam and away from Melanie, their conversation picking up and roaming over past events shared by the four of them. Events that Melanie had no part in.

And once again Melanie felt as if she was on the outside looking in.

Would they even notice if she left? Would they care?

Melanie brushed the questions away as she waited for the right moment to leave. She didn't need to see the approval that Tom and Amanda so easily bestowed on Sandy and withheld from her, a stranger.

So much of her life had been spent yearning to be a part of a family. As Sandy was.

And what did she have to compare to this family gathering? Her mother's grave in the Derwin cemetery and a father who had chosen to be cremated.

Compared to Sandy and the rich heritage she had in the family surrounding them, she was a pauper.

"I'm going to check on Tiffany a moment," she said to Adam. The longer she stayed with them, the more excluded she would feel. She wasn't an insecure young girl anymore who sought approval from those who spurned her.

Adam made a move to stop her, but was waylaid by Tom, and, without looking back to see Adam's reaction, Melanie left.

Chapter Fourteen

◆

She was walking down the road. He could see her figure moving between the trees that shielded the Gerrard property from the graveled road.

The tension holding Adam's shoulders in its fierce grip dissipated as he started jogging down the driveway. He had left Tom and Amanda as soon as he could, but Melanie had disappeared. His mother hadn't seen her, nor had Mr. Matheson.

"Melanie, wait," he called out as he came onto the road.

She hesitated, then turned, waiting as he caught up.

"I thought you left," he said, breathless with the unexpected exertion. "Then I saw your car was still parked here."

"It's blocked off." A light breeze played with her hair, tossing it about her face. She pushed it back, tucking it behind her ear, her eyes avoiding his.

"Why did you leave?"

She looked away, over the open spaces beyond the

road, as if she might find the reason there. "I knew I shouldn't have come, Adam. I don't belong here."

"I'm sorry about Amanda," Adam said, wanting to reach out and take her in his arms. But so much had happened so quickly, he still wasn't sure what her reaction would be and what would be appropriate on his part. "She's always been an overly protective mother. I suspect that might have been part of Lana's problem, as well. And part of the reason I blamed myself."

"You know better, don't you?" Melanie's eyes were pleading. And once again her hand lay on his arm, warm, hopeful.

Adam let his gaze travel over her face. Her touch encouraged him. He gave in to an impulse and eased a strand of hair away from her forehead. "The psalm the minister read this morning was the same one my mother read to me last night. 'Restore unto me the joy of Thy salvation.' I didn't have that joy because I blamed God. I blamed God because I always thought Amanda blamed me. Because I thought she was right." He caressed her cheek with his knuckle, his feelings for her still a confusion. "And thanks to what you told me, I realized it wasn't true. Lana made her own choices."

Melanie smiled up at him, her lips trembling. "I'm glad, Adam. I'm glad you let God set you free from what you were dragging around."

"God set me free, but so did you." He lowered his hand to her neck, grazing her collarbone with his thumb. Then he slipped his hand around her back and drew her carefully to him, holding her close.

She came willingly into his arms. Slipped her own around him.

Adam sighed into her hair, his chin resting on her head. He knew he was falling in love with her.

And he knew he didn't want to leave.

Melanie drew in a deep breath, smoothed down her skirt and knocked on the office door of the new superintendent.

"Come in," Tanya Docker called out.

Melanie sent up a prayer, and stepped into the office.

Tanya was standing at the desk frowning at a file folder open in front of her.

"Sit down, please, Melanie," Tanya said, indicating with her pen the empty chair on the other side of the desk. She sat down herself, granting Melanie a quick glance. "Glad you could come in." She adjusted her blazer, touched her hair with an absent gesture, her eyes still on the papers in front of her.

"Your work here has been exemplary and your references are very good."

Only a deaf person would have missed the "but" in her voice, Melanie thought, swallowing a knot of fear. She waited, however, still hopeful.

Tanya sighed and looked directly at Melanie for the first time. "But I'm afraid the full-time position is no longer available."

Melanie heard the words, saw the regret on Tanya's face, yet it seemed to take long seconds before they registered completely.

Ice slipped through her veins, deadening her.

"How…" It was all she could get past her suddenly dry lips.

Tanya Docker flipped her file closed with her index finger and folded her hands on top of it. Not one gray hair was out of place, and her blazer didn't even bunch at the shoulders from sitting down. She looked as efficient as she sounded. "Our budget has been cut back substantially, and we've had to take away the full-time position you had applied for."

It was as if a hand of lead pushed down on her shoulders. "When did…" She stopped, trying to catch her composure, and tried again. "When did this information come your way?"

Tanya didn't meet her eye, simply ran her finger slowly up and down the edge of the file. "I found out two weeks ago. This was the earliest I could tell you. I'm sorry. I'm sure it can't be easy."

"I banked on that job." She thought of her loan and winced at her word usage. "I just made an offer on a house…."

Tanya held her hands up as if soothing a troubled child. "I'm sorry to tell you this. I'm sure it can't be easy."

Melanie unclenched her fists. Drew in a deep breath. "Is there anyone else I can speak to about this?" she asked, thankful that her voice sounded more steady than she felt. "The department head? The director of the Health Authority?"

"I'm afraid not. The decision to make the cut was done by the Health Region."

"My current job officially terminates the end of this week. I don't suppose there's any way it could be extended." It was such a faint hope, and the gentle shaking of Tanya's head extinguished it before it could even settle.

"I'm really sorry, Melanie. You're an excellent nurse. All your reports have been exemplary and I hate to lose you, but…" Tanya lifted her hands in a limp gesture of resignation. "I hope you can find something else on such short notice. We will be giving you a glowing recommendation, of course."

Melanie listened with one part of her mind as realization hit the other. No wonder her loan wasn't approved. The bank had known her job was in jeopardy before she did.

What was she going to do now?

Find another job. Move. But which one would happen first? And how did Adam fit into all of this? Yesterday he had made some faint noises about staying in Derwin. For a brief, luminous moment, she'd thought maybe something would happen.

But now?

"So again, I'm sorry, Melanie," Tanya continued.

Melanie forced herself to smile. To respond. As soon as was reasonably polite she was out the door and then, thankfully, outside.

She made it to her car without stumbling, without tears. When she got inside, she waited for the anger to come. She had wanted this house so long and now the opportunity had been snatched away.

She thought of Adam. Wondered what would happen between them. Because no matter how she looked at the situation, she knew she was falling in love with him.

Yet nothing had been settled. Their relationship was too uncertain. They needed time that neither was going to get. By the end of the week she had to find another job, probably in another town, and by the end of next week Adam was moving back to Calgary.

Could I go with him if he asked?

What if he didn't ask?

She pressed her fist against her forehead, swallowing down the tears of confusion that pressed behind her eyes. *I need Your help to get through this, Lord. Show me what I have to do.*

Her scattered prayer twisted and pulled as she tried to focus, one thought, one idea surfacing with icy clarity.

Her dream house had once again become just a dream.

I'm not going to be living here, Melanie thought, pulling up to the Engler home half an hour later. She had repeated the words to herself again and again as she drove, hoping that by the time she got to the house, reality and thoughts would have meshed.

Her heart still twisted, however, when she saw the familiar lines of the house. In spite of her brave words to herself, she still felt the pull of the house, a sense of homecoming that would never happen.

She didn't have an appointment scheduled for Helen this morning, but her other client had canceled, leaving the morning open. But now, as she parked in front of the house, her emotions were a confusion of disappointment and excitement at the possibility of seeing Adam again.

And even that bright hope held a touch of the bittersweet. Nothing was settled between them, in spite of her growing feelings for him. And his changing relationship with God.

"Melanie, we're over here," Helen called out, waving to Melanie from the backyard. Tiffany was crouching down some distance away from Adam, who looked to be digging in one of the flower beds.

Her eyes clung to him as she walked up to them, her heartbeat as light and precarious as the flight of a butterfly.

He turned as she came near, his smile lighting up his face. "What a nice surprise," he said, standing up. "I was going to leave a message for you, but now I don't have to."

"I wasn't supposed to come today," Melanie said, unable to keep her eyes off him, wondering what his message was. "I got a cancellation and thought I would stop by. It was such a nice day." She was babbling, and she clamped her lips together.

Adam's smile widened. For a moment Melanie thought he might give her a quick hug, but all he did was slap the sides of his jeans to brush the dirt off his hands. "Mom was just supervising some planting. We got some perennials at half price at the nursery this morning. Thought they would brighten the yard up."

Melanie couldn't help but compare the yard to when she'd first come here. Then it had looked like an unorganized garage sale. Now it welcomed you to sit down. Contemplate life. And now Adam was putting in perennials?

"Looks very nice." She tried to inject a note of enthusiasm into her voice, but without success.

Adam seemed to sense her mood. He angled her a questioning glance but she looked away, watching Tiffany digging up the dirt with her shovel, oblivious to what was going on. Lucky child.

"Well, let's have some lemonade," Helen said, turning her walker around. "I just made some. Tiffany, you can come with me to put the glasses out."

Tiffany dropped her shovel and noticed Melanie for the first time. "Melanie," she called out, running toward her as she always did.

And as she always did, Melanie dropped down to catch the little bundle of warm humanity. Tiffany smelled like dirt and orange Popsicle and felt like love. Melanie clung to her, a pang of sorrow piercing her. She cared for this little child more than she had realized.

"You're squishing me, Melanie," Tiffany complained.

"I'm sorry," Melanie said, reluctantly lowering her to the ground. Then as she straightened, she realized what Tiffany had said. "She said my name the right way," she said to Adam.

"We've been practicing." Adam gave Melanie a quick wink. "Thought she better learn to say it right."

She wondered what he meant by that. Then wondered if she had read too much into his light comment. Then wondered why she wondered.

Her head was spinning.

"So what are you doing?"

"Helping my daddy and gramma plant plants." Tiffany pressed her finger to her orange-rimmed mouth. "It's a secret. For you."

"Tiffany, are you coming?" Helen called from the step.

"I go help Gramma," Tiffany announced, and without a backward glance bounced off toward the house.

When the door banged shut behind her, Melanie turned to Adam, unnerved to find him only inches away from her.

"Hey, there," he said quietly, the timbre of his voice creating intimacy in the open space surrounding them. He grazed her cheek with his knuckle. "I'm glad you came."

His touch weakened her knees and undermined her resolve. She wanted answers, but she didn't know which questions to ask. Once she had asked him what was happening between them and he hadn't been able to answer her. And she had only been able to tell him that she couldn't consider a relationship with someone who didn't want to have a relationship with God.

Yesterday she had seen a different side of Adam. Had sat beside him in church and knew for a fact that he had been touched by God.

And now she didn't know where to go. In the past twenty-four hours her whole life had turned topsy-turvy and she didn't know which constant to cling to.

Only God's love.

She took a deep breath at that gentle reminder.

"I have something to tell you," she said quietly, looking away. She might as well get this part over and done with. "I just found out this morning that I didn't get the job I was hoping to get. I talked to Floyd on the way here. I'm withdrawing my offer to buy the house."

Adam went completely still.

A gentle breeze sifted through the leaves of the trembling aspen and chased a scrap of paper across the yard as the silence stretched out.

"I'm sorry, Melanie," Adam said quietly. "I know how much this house meant to you."

Melanie only nodded, then looked up at him. "It did. I guess it was just a dream after all."

"So now what happens for you, Melanie?"

Was that her call to make? What about Adam? So now what happens for him?

She wrapped her fingers around each other, tilted her shoulder up as she glanced up at him. "I have to find another job somewhere else."

Adam's frown darkened his face. "Where would you go?"

His answer wasn't heartening and she answered with a vague movement of her hands. "Wherever I can get work. I'm going to have to start looking as soon as possible. My job is over this week."

"So soon?"

"What are you going to do about the house?" she asked. She didn't want to talk about herself anymore. It was depressing.

"I'm not sure." He blew out his breath and caught the back of his neck in a gesture that Melanie now recognized as tension. "My partner phoned this morning asking when I was going to get the money from you. I guess that isn't going to happen.''

This was getting more and more awkward, Melanie thought. Each dancing around their feelings, not sure what to commit to. Unsure of where the other stood.

''Melanie, I need to...''

The beeper going off at her side stopped Adam midsentence. Melanie glanced at the number, angry at the intrusion.

It was the clinic. They could wait.

''I'm sorry, Adam. What were you going to say?''

He shook his head. ''It can wait. Make your phone call.''

It was her supervisor. One of her patients needed her to come immediately. Could Melanie go?

She didn't want to, but her patient's care came first. ''I'm sorry,'' she said to Adam when she'd put away her cell phone. ''I've got to go.''

''Of course you do.'' He waited a moment, then, to her utter surprise, bent over and brushed his lips lightly over hers. ''I'll come and see you tonight.''

More confusion, and yet a promise. He was going to see her tonight.

And as she drove away, her heart sang.

''I don't know if I like the layout.'' Eileen Olson turned around in the kitchen, her arms folded around her waist, her lips pursed. ''We'd need to put all new cupboards in.''

''The foundation is solid,'' Floyd said, ''and Adam redid the wiring. Anything you would need to do would be superficial.''

Adam stifled his annoyance with Eileen and Floyd. When Melanie had delivered her bomb, his first reaction was disappointment for her. He knew how badly she wanted this house.

Then, on the heels of that came the realization that she was free of this obligation. She could go where she wanted. And that's what scared him.

Then Floyd had called saying that he had an older couple who were interested in the house.

Kyle had phoned this morning asking him about the money and he had put him off. He didn't want to go back to Calgary.

"The living room needs a paint job," Eileen was saying, listing off yet more negatives. "I just don't know." She turned to her husband. "What do you think?"

"We've hardly seen the whole house, Eileen," he said. "I'm not ready to make a call yet."

"Adam, why don't you show them the master bedroom?" Floyd said. "It's one of the finished rooms in the house, and will give you a good idea of what the rest of the house might look like with a little bit of work."

"A lot of work," Eileen added.

Adam was starting to get annoyed. When they had walked around the outside of the house, Adam had been honest, but fair. The exterior did need work and he'd pointed out what needed to be done. He had done the same with Melanie only a few weeks ago.

But somehow when she was looking at it, she could see beyond the blistering paint, the worn-out eaves troughs to what it would look like if someone who cared about it spent some time.

Adam opened the door to the master bedroom and stepped aside as Eileen and her husband, Jerry, entered.

They were silent. Eileen walked around his mother's bed to the windows. She twitched the curtains aside, her mouth still pulled tight like a drawstring purse.

"This is a lovely room," Jerry said, standing in the doorway. "Just beautiful."

"Not too bad," Eileen sniffed.

The room was beautiful and they knew it. This was a waste of time.

But Floyd chivvied them along, bringing them upstairs. Adam showed them the rooms one at a time, growing more defensive by the minute as Mrs. Olson consistently found things wrong with the house.

It was a good place. It would make a lovely home.

"I can't show you the attic. The stairs broke a while ago and I haven't bothered to replace them," Adam said as he opened the door to the last room upstairs. The room directly above his mother's bedroom.

Again Eileen was the first to enter. Again she walked straight to the window. She stopped, her hands resting on the sill, and for the first time she had nothing to say.

Jerry came alongside her. "What a beautiful view," he said quietly.

Adam remembered Melanie standing in the same place. The gentle smile on her face as she'd revealed her memories and dreams to him. Her love for this house and the family that had occupied it. And at that time his emotions had been in such a negative state he'd felt as if he had to disabuse her of her illusions. Let her know that this was not a place to pin so much hope on.

But so much had changed since then. Listening to Eileen Olson talk so negatively about a house that Melanie had yearned so deeply for shifted his own perspective.

He didn't think they were going to buy it, but even if they did, he didn't know if he wanted to sell it to them. Or anyone.

He wanted to keep it. For himself.

The thought dived into his soul and made a home there.

He didn't want to go back to Calgary and Kyle and fourteen-hour work days. He wanted a home for his daughter. And he wanted Melanie in it.

And he wanted it here. In Derwin.

The realization struck him with an uplifting rush of joy.

Eileen turned away from the window and saw the dresser Adam had built for Melanie.

"Where did that come from?" she asked, running her fingers over the top. "This is a fine piece of workmanship."

"I made it," Adam said.

She pulled open a drawer and pulled out some cards. "What are these?"

"Paint chips, it looks like," Floyd said.

"They're labeled." Eileen waved them at Adam. "Did you choose these?"

Adam stifled a flux of resentment. Those belonged to Melanie. "Someone else was thinking of purchasing the house. She had chosen those colors for the various rooms and the exterior."

Eileen shuffled through them. "She has good taste. The colors she has chosen are amazing." She found the one for the room they were in and held it up, nodding. "I think I can visualize what she wanted to accomplish here. Very lovely." She slapped them against her hand as she turned a full circle in the room. "Can I keep them?"

"Of course you can," Floyd said. "The person who picked those out isn't going to be buying the house."

"They were in the dresser," Adam said, flashing a warning look at Floyd. "They belong to the owner."

"I thought you owned the dresser?" Eileen's voice held a peeved note. As if unused to being turned down.

"No. I made it for Melanie Visser. It's hers."

"Well, then, I guess they stay here." Eileen dropped the cards carelessly on top of the dresser and walked out of the room in a huff. Jerry followed.

Floyd waited until they were out of earshot, then turned to Adam, glowering. "What are you doing? She was starting to come around. Why couldn't she have those lousy paint chips?"

"They don't belong to me." They were part of Melanie's dream and he was loath to part with even a small part of it.

Floyd frowned at Adam, his arms folded across his chest. "Okay, Adam. What's happening? My first prospective buyer you almost scare off with a list of repairs that would have stymied anyone less determined than Melanie. Now you're going to ruin a prospective sale over a bunch of lousy paint chips that you can pick up at the hardware store for nothing?"

Adam just shrugged. "I don't think those paint chips are going to swing this deal for you, Floyd." He walked out of the room without a backward glance.

Ten minutes later he was standing on the porch watching Floyd drive off with the Olsons.

He didn't think he would hear from them again.

Tomorrow he would phone Floyd and officially pull the listing off the market, which would release him from the agreement he'd signed with Floyd. The house was no longer for sale. For now, he had other things to do.

And twenty-five minutes later he was standing in the hallway of Melanie's apartment, knocking on her door, his heart keeping heavy time with his fist.

The door opened with a faint creak and Melanie stood in front of him, backlit by the sun coming in through her patio doors.

Adam swallowed at the sight of her, easily calling back yesterday when she was in his arms and he felt as if his life was slowly moving toward a still center.

And now?

How did he start? What questions were his right to ask?

"Can I come in?"

She nodded and stood aside, still clinging to the door like a shield. She closed it behind him and stayed there.

"Floyd brought some people to the house today," he said, stringing his thumbs in the belt loops of his jeans as he noted the piled-up empty boxes in the living room. "Potential buyers."

Melanie's gaze skittered down and away and he caught a glimpse of sorrow. She nodded, leaning against the door as if drawing strength from it. "What did they think of the house?"

"Not much. I don't think they're going to take it."

She just nodded.

The awkwardness that had been so palpable this afternoon was back. He had come here full of expectation, yet now that he stood in front of her, the woman he knew he was in love with, he didn't know how to articulate his feelings. So much had changed.

This afternoon he'd found himself looking with different eyes at a house he had once wanted to dump as quickly as possible. Now he began to see it as a home.

For him and Melanie.

"Do you want to move?" he asked, still unsure, still cautious.

As Melanie shook her head, he caught the glint of a tear in her eyes. "Of course not."

"Melanie, I don't want you to leave."

She looked back at him, her incredulous gaze holding his. "Leave what?"

Adam dared to close the distance between them, to

gently take her in his arms once again. Like a home-coming.

He drew her close, resting his chin on her head, taking a chance now that she was in his arms. "I don't want you to leave me, Melanie. I don't need any more time to think about it."

She melted against him, her arms slipping around his waist as they had yesterday, her damp cheeks pressed against his shoulder. "I don't want to go, either."

His eyes drifted shut as he held her close. "Thank You, Lord," he whispered.

She drew back just enough to see his face. "You came to church yesterday. And now you're praying." She stopped there, as if hoping he would finish her thoughts.

"I tried to ignore God, Melanie, but He didn't ignore me. Like those letters Jason had sent his wife, the love was there, waiting. I just needed to read it. To listen." He wiped a glistening track of moisture from her cheek with his thumb, glorious happiness welling up in him like a fountain. "I know I'm not there yet, but I also know that if I seek Him, I will find Him." He touched his lips to her forehead, then her cheek.

He kissed her again and held her close, wonder and amazement flooding through him like a cleansing stream that had accumulated drop by drop until this afternoon. When he knew he didn't want to sell the house. He wanted it for himself and Melanie and Tiffany and his mother.

"Are you busy tomorrow night?" he said suddenly. "Can you come for supper?" He had to get some plans in place and for that he needed time.

"Sure. I'd like that." Her smile was all the encouragement he needed. He kissed her again. "Then we'll see you tomorrow." He didn't know if he could wait. But he knew that for the first time in years, his life was moving in a good direction.

Chapter Fifteen

"**W**here are we going?" Melanie asked. Supper was over, the dishes done and Adam had drawn her aside, telling her that he had something he wanted to say. In private. Just then the phone started ringing.

"I'll get it," Helen said, smiling a benevolent smile.

She knew, Adam thought. But nothing could stifle his happiness now.

"Just follow me." Adam turned to Melanie, took her hand and led her up the stairs, then turned to the left and opened the upper tower room.

He let her precede him and she stepped inside, looking around, unsure of where this was going. The first thing she saw was her dresser—but surely that wasn't what he wanted to show her?

"You moved this up here for nothing," she said wistfully, running her hand over the smooth surface.

Adam caught her hand and lifted it to his lips. "No, I don't think I did." He walked backward, drawing her toward the window. Once there, he pulled her into his arms. "And look, the sun is obliging me with just the right tone."

Pink and orange splashed on the underside of the clouds, reflected in the pond beyond the fenced-in yard.

"Obliging you with what?" Melanie asked. Where was he going with all this?

Adam gently brushed her hair back from her face, his eyes following his hand. His fingers trembled.

"I wish I knew where to start. The first time I saw you, all those years ago, I had a feeling about you. That you were someone special. Now, as I've gotten to know you, I've learned that my intuition was right. You have a beauty of spirit, a generous heart and a faith that I've learned much from."

Melanie swallowed down a flutter of anticipation. He sounded so serious. Intent.

Adam's hand cupped her chin as his wonderfully blue eyes delved into hers. "You've given me hope and encouragement. You've set my feet on right paths. For the first time in years I feel like I'm moving in a good direction. Closer to God, closer to family. Closer to you." He paused, his thumb lightly caressing her chin, his voice growing softer. "I don't want to move away. I don't want you to move away, either. I want to stay here. In Derwin. In this house. With you."

Melanie held his gaze, his last words resonating through all the lonely places of her life and filling them with a joy so great she thought she would burst.

Adam slipped his hand into the pocket of his pants and pulled out a small velvet box.

"I know it's a little soon, but I was afraid to wait."

Melanie's heart did double time as he opened it. A diamond solitaire sparkled back at her from the depths of the velvet box.

"Will you marry me?"

Such simple words. And what a storm they created in her heart. She reached up to touch his face, as if to catch his words and hold them to herself.

Her dream. Come true.

"Yes. I will" was all she could say.

And suddenly she was in his arms, held close to a heart beating in time with hers.

And as they kissed, she felt, for the first time in years, as if she had finally come home.

"A toast," Helen said, lifting up her glass when they eventually came back downstairs. "To Melanie and Adam. Long life and good health. May God's blessing fall on you in all the places of your life."

Adam accepted his mother's blessing with a smile that wouldn't quit. He didn't think his heart could take in one more ounce of happiness. He looked around the table and he raised his own glass. "And I want to propose a toast to the three most important women in my life." He turned to Helen. "My mother. Faithful in prayer and love." Then to Tiffany. "My daughter, a blessing from God that I hope to never take for granted." Finally he turned to Melanie. "And to my future wife. The woman who brought me back home."

Melanie raised her glass and touched Adam's, the diamond on her finger sparkling almost as brightly as her amber eyes. "And to you, Adam. First among men and first in my life. Here's to many years together," she returned, her voice husky. "Many, many years."

Her added words took on a rare poignancy. They both knew what she meant. "May God bless us," he whispered, touching his glass to hers.

Adam looked around the table, unable to stop smiling. He knew he didn't deserve this happiness, but at the same time he had learned how guilt had kept him from enjoying the good things God had given him. He was simply going to allow God to work His way in their lives. And trust that His love would carry them through.

"Did I hear a vehicle?" Helen said, cocking her head to one side. Then she clapped her hand to her head. "In all the excitement, I forgot to tell you that Floyd is coming over."

Voices drifted up the walk, footsteps echoed in the darkness.

A knock on the back door.

Adam turned on the porch light. Floyd stood in profile to the door talking to Eileen and Jerry Olson.

"Adam. Sorry to disturb you," Floyd turned, his smile more generous than it had been yesterday. "As I told your mother, Mr. and Mrs. Olson want to take another look through the house. They're having some second thoughts."

Adam stifled his annoyance. In his excitement he'd forgotten to tell Floyd the house was off the market.

But he didn't want to look ungracious, so he stepped aside to allow them in. He would pull Floyd aside and tell him at the first opportunity.

"Hello, Melanie. Good to see you again." Floyd reached across the table to shake her hand, his smile even wider. He turned to the Olsons. "Melanie, I'd like you to meet Eileen and Jerry Olson. They're considering buying this place. Helen and Tiffany, you've met the Olsons already?" He didn't give Helen a chance to answer, but turned to Eileen. "Melanie is the former buyer who had picked out the colors you admired."

Melanie threw a puzzled glance Adam's way. He shook his head. He'd explain later. For now they just had to go through the formalities.

"I have to say, I was very impressed with your color combinations," Eileen was saying to Melanie. "Gave me second thoughts about the house. I'm so glad you're here. I'd like to know what else you were planning on doing here."

"Eileen saw the paint chips you had sitting in the dresser upstairs," Adam put in.

Melanie nodded, but Adam could see she was still not sure what was going on.

"I hope we're not interrupting anything," Jerry said, hanging back, obviously uncomfortable.

"Just a small celebration," Helen replied, adjusting her glasses.

Adam laid a quieting hand on his mother's shoulder. The last time the Olsons had been here Helen had taken quite personally Eileen's disparaging comments about the house. Who knew what she might say.

"Really, what are you celebrating?" Floyd asked.

"Adam and Melanie's engagement," Helen said, her voice prim.

Congratulations were murmured, and Floyd gave Adam a knowing look. Adam was uncomfortable with the attention. He didn't want all these people around during this special moment. He wished his mother had passed on Floyd's message sooner. He would have told Floyd not to come over.

Floyd turned to the Olsons. "So you've seen the house already—would you like to go through it again?"

"I'd like Melanie to show us through," Eileen said. "If you don't mind."

"No. I don't mind." Melanie spoke slowly, a puzzled frown creasing her forehead.

And why wouldn't she be confused? Just moments before he had told her they were going to be making their home in Derwin. In this house. Now she was being asked to show a prospective buyer through it.

"Where would you like to start?" Melanie asked, getting up from the table.

"This kitchen." Eileen waved her hand around the room they were standing in. "What would you do about the cabinets?"

Melanie ran her hand along the edge of the cabinets. "They need to be sanded down and painted. I was looking at a pale cream with sage-green trim."

Eileen nodded, her lips pursed as she considered

what Melanie was telling her. "Why not new cup-boards?"

"These fit with the decor and I like the country-style kitchen rather than the more modern U shape or island separating the cabinets from the rest of the kitchen. You get better flow between table and counter." Melanie smiled, glancing over her shoulder at Adam. "It creates a more family-centered atmosphere."

Adam felt her gaze as tangible as a touch.

He and Floyd and Jerry followed Melanie and Eileen into the front room. The male entourage, Adam thought. Cut out of the loop because they couldn't interpret the difference between eggshell, cream and off-white.

"I don't know if I like the fireplace," Eileen said, tapping her finger against her lips as they stood in the empty front room. "What were you going to do with it?"

"I had thought of an insert." Melanie walked over to the mantel and straightened a picture of Adam and Tiffany that she and Helen had put up there. Again her hands lingered on the picture, brushed a small bit of dust off the mantel. "That would make it more energy efficient."

"But the mess."

Melanie smiled and waved her objections away. "The ambience of a truly warm place in the house outweighs the disadvantages. Besides, it's a great place to dry up mittens when kids come in from playing in the snow."

Eileen nodded, as if to picture it.

Melanie took them through the rest of the house, pointing out the advantages. The oak newel post and banister that just needed the paint stripped off to show their true beauty. How the light coming in from the window in the landing could be enhanced with the insertion of a stained glass window. Why she wouldn't replace the carpet in the upstairs hallway, but would take down the wallpaper, and how much lighter it would be.

And as Melanie told Eileen her plans for the house, Adam found himself falling in love with his own house. He found resurrected his own plans and dreams for this place that was to be a home.

And he loved her all the more for it. He could picture other children in the bedrooms. See Melanie and himself tucking children into beds, before going downstairs to sit in front of a fire in the fireplace.

A family in a home that he had once wanted to get rid of. But best of all, a family with Melanie at his side.

He wanted the Olsons gone. He wanted to go through the house with Melanie himself. He wanted to dream aloud with his arm around her.

As Melanie was leading them back down the stairs again, Adam pulled Floyd aside. "I have to talk to you."

Floyd gestured for Melanie and the Olsons to go ahead, then turned to Adam. "What is it?"

"The house is not for sale, Floyd. I forgot to phone you and tell you. I'm pulling it off the market."

Floyd shook his head, his smile regretful. "Sorry, Adam. I can't do that. I have an interested party."

"But I haven't signed anything yet."

"You signed an agreement with me, Adam. And I have a party that is serious. Finances aren't going to be a problem for them." Floyd lifted his hands in a gesture of resignation. "You could back me on it and maybe I'd give in. But Olson has a legal right here." And with those heartening words he followed the Olson's into the kitchen.

"Thank you, Melanie, that was very helpful." Eileen looked around the kitchen again, a smile on her face. "This house would make a lovely home. I think I've fallen in love with it." She turned to Floyd. "We'll take it."

Adam's heart plummeted.

And as he caught Melanie's puzzled look, he wondered how he was going to tell her that for the second time in only two days she had lost this house.

Melanie closed the door to Tiffany's room and turned to Adam standing behind her. "How quickly things change," she said softly, drifting into the haven of his arms. "Just goes to show you that there are no certainties in life."

"I'm so sorry, Melanie." Adam held her close. Pressed a kiss to her head. "I didn't think they were going to buy it. I feel like I've lost your dream for you."

"No. Don't say that." She drew her head back to look into his deep blue eyes. "You've given me better dreams. Better plans. You had said at one time that I was putting too much on this house." She glanced down the hallway at the window she had pointed out to Eileen. "You were right. I made this house my source of happiness. And I should have known better."

Adam brushed a light kiss over her forehead. "I guess we'll have to look somewhere else for a place, then."

"In Calgary?"

"Would that bother you?"

Melanie smiled, then smoothed the frown away from his forehead. "I'll go where you go. Even it if means moving all the way to Calgary."

"I don't think we'll have to do that," he said, stroking her cheek. "I've been talking to Graydon. I think he wants a partner. And I think I want to be that partner." His expression grew serious. "I want to stay here, Melanie, in spite of the memories."

"We can make better ones," she said, her heart soaring.

"I like this one better than the newer one." Melanie looked around the yard of the small house Floyd had shown her previously, trying to imagine Tiffany playing in the backyard. Pansies spilled out of the flower beds along the house and behind them the last few tiger lilies nodded in the summer breeze. "It has a nice big yard and it's close to the school. Tiffany will be able to walk there." She walked over to the apple tree, pleased to see tiny apples developing.

"We could add to the house some day." Adam folded his arms as he studied the house. "It's in better shape than my house is."

"I like the country kitchen."

He turned to Melanie. "The other house was bigger. Are you sure you want this one?"

"I am." She sat down on the bench at the base of the apple tree and looked around the yard with a pleased smile. This would make a lovely home. She felt a momentary pang for the loss of her other dream, but she pushed it aside. She had Adam. Tiffany. Helen.

And God's love covering them all.

She truly needed nothing more.

"This house has personality," she said with a smile.

"Okay, what story is attached to this house?" he teased, nudging her aside with his hip.

"Let's see." Melanie hugged her knees, angling Adam a mischievous glance. "The owner used to be a single woman. Everything she had, she put into this house. It was her dream home."

"Aah. I think I know this story."

"Maybe you do. Maybe you don't. Anyway, one day a man came selling magazine subscriptions. He talked her into subscribing to a magazine about moving back to the land. They fell in love and he whisked her away to a mountain hideaway where she makes cinnamon rolls every other day and is learning to milk a goat."

"Sounds like a fairy story to me," he said with a wry smile.

"Don't be cynical." She turned to him, catching his hands in hers. "There's all kinds of happy endings in real life. Just depends on where you end the story."

"That one I would have quit at the whisking part."

He pulled her to her feet. "And this story isn't finished, so if we are serious about this place, I guess we should go talk to Floyd. We have to be there anyhow to sign the Agreement for Sale on my place, so we better get going."

Melanie took another look around the yard, trying not to compare it to the home that had absorbed so many daydreams. It was a lovely place and it would be their home. And she and Adam and Tiffany would make their own dreams in it.

The real estate office was only a couple of blocks away, so they walked there holding hands like a young couple. Melanie felt a gentle peace suffuse her as they walked past other homes, down a street sheltered by sweeping poplar trees and stately spruce. It was an established neighborhood with history and character.

Thank you, Lord, she prayed. *Thank You for giving me more than I need. Help us to make a home here.*

Floyd was busy with another client when they came into the office, so they sat down to wait in the reception area.

Melanie tapped her fingers together, suddenly restless and edgy, just as she was when she was ready to sign the Agreement for Sale for the Engler house.

She wanted to get this over and done with so she and Adam could get back to their wedding plans. And their plans for their future.

Adam was going to go back to work for Graydon, and had been spending as much time arranging that as they had trying to find a new home.

Melanie had managed to obtain another part-time

contract with the Health Authority and she was satisfied with that. She had Tiffany now to take care of, and she didn't want to miss out on any part of her development.

She got up and walked once around the reception area, giving the secretary a vague smile. Other houses were listed on the board by the desk and she took a moment to look them over.

"Second thoughts?" Adam murmured over the top of his magazine.

She shook her head. It didn't matter where she and Adam lived. They would be together.

A shadow fell across the door and Melanie glanced over. Her heart clenched.

It was the Olsons, come to take care of the final bit of business.

Eileen gave Melanie a wan smile, then sat down. Jerry sat beside Adam, said a brief hello and dived into a magazine.

"Well, I see we're all here." Floyd bustled into the room, spilling energy and good cheer into the silence. "Come into my office and we can get the final bit of business cleared up." He stood aside as the Olsons walked down the hallway ahead of Melanie and Adam.

"So what did you think of the house, Adam?" Floyd asked as they settled into his office.

"Melanie and I both like it. Nice location." He shrugged. "What else can I say?"

"So you'll probably take it?"

"Probably."

"Excellent." Floyd almost rubbed his hands together.

He should be pleased, Melanie thought as she settled into the chair. Two sales in one day. Exit one dream, enter another.

"Are you looking at purchasing another place?" Eileen asked.

Melanie only nodded, wrapping her fingers around each other.

"In town?"

"Yes. A lovely little home only a few blocks from here." She had to say more than yes or run the risk of looking ungracious.

"I see." Eileen unzipped her purse, then zipped it up again. "I understand from Floyd that you withdrew your offer on the house because you didn't get a job you had applied for."

Melanie shot Floyd an annoyed glance. He just lifted his hands in a feeble apology.

"That's correct," Melanie said. "Although I just found out I will be getting a part-time position in a month."

Eileen just nodded.

"So I have the papers ready here," Floyd said, leaning over the desk. "All we have to do is get signatures and the deal is done. Pending financing, of course."

"That won't be a problem," Jerry said. He pulled the paper toward him and skimmed it. He was about to pick up the pen when Eileen put her hand on his.

"Don't sign it yet," she said, sounding breathless.

Eileen turned to Melanie. "The house we're buying. You love it, don't you?"

Why is she doing this to me? thought Melanie. She only nodded.

"I could tell that. When you showed us around." Eileen chewed her lower lip, wearing away her red lipstick. "I could tell that you wanted it badly."

Melanie swallowed, then felt Adam's hand on her shoulder. He squeezed as if in encouragement. And it reminded her of what was important.

"It was a dream of mine," she said quietly, looking over at her future husband. "I wanted that house for a home, but I realized that wherever Adam and I will be, that will be our home."

"I think you will be able to do that." Eileen's smile was bittersweet. "I have to confess I didn't want the house at all. And neither did Jerry. Until you showed me around. You made me fall in love with it. And if you could do that, it made me wonder how much that house meant to you." Eileen glanced over at her husband. "Jerry is willing to indulge me, but I know he doesn't really want to live that far out of town."

Hope stirred briefly in Melanie's soul, but she pushed it down. "It isn't that far away," Melanie said, trying again to show them the positives.

Eileen laid her hand on Melanie's. "Bless you, my dear. Still trying to sell it." She withdrew her hand and straightened. "But it won't work." She turned to Floyd. "We're withdrawing our offer. I don't want to buy the house anymore."

Floyd dropped his pen onto the desk with a clatter.

"Don't be too hasty," he said. "The house is a great buy. Look at it as an investment."

The faint hope that had stirred in Melanie grew. Filled her as Eileen continued.

"Once Melanie showed me the house I could see the potential. I was starting to see that house as a showpiece," Eileen said with a touch of pride. "Something I could show off to my friends. It could be a good investment and I'm sure we would get a good return." Eileen turned to Melanie with a smile that made the hope blossom fully. "But I know for you it will be a home."

"Thank you," Melanie whispered, engulfed with joy.

"Do you mind, Jerry?" Eileen glanced at her husband apologetically.

"Fine by me." Jerry spoke up. He stood up, obviously wanting to put a quick end to this. "Floyd, sorry about all this, but thanks for your time. Adam, thanks again. Best wishes on your wedding, Melanie." He turned to his wife. "Eileen, let's go." And with those abrupt pronouncements, he left.

Eileen turned at the doorway. "Melanie, send me a picture once you've got the outside painted. I'd love to see what you've done with it."

Melanie blinked, trying to assimilate what had happened, then understood what she'd said. "Sure. I'll do that." She gave Eileen a vague smile, then turned to Adam.

"Did I understand this right?"

"I think so." Adam's smile was as big as hers.

Floyd sat back in his chair, shaking his head, a

dazed expression on his face. "I can't believe this. Two commissions. Gone. In minutes. The other Realtors will never believe me." He turned to Melanie. "I don't suppose you'll be buying the little house."

She gave him a look filled with regret and shook her head.

"And you don't need to buy Adam's house." He pushed himself away from his desk, emitting a sigh. "Maybe the Olsons might be interested in the little house." He turned to Adam and Melanie. "Well, thanks for the interesting ride. It's been, well, interesting." He shook Adam's hand, then Melanie's. "And I expect to be invited to the wedding."

"I'm sure we can arrange that," Melanie said.

The walk back to the truck was made in silence. As if each had to absorb what had just happened. But then, as Adam unlocked the door for Melanie, she stopped him.

"Did that really just happen?" she said, still trying to comprehend it all.

Adam canted his head to one side, studying her. "From the looks of things, I'm back where I started. Can't get rid of it, can I?"

"Do you want to?"

Adam ran his knuckle down her cheek, then cupped the back of her head in his hand. "I want to make a home there. With you and Tiffany. With God as its head. That's what I want."

And as he drew her into his arms, Melanie sent up a prayer of thankfulness and happiness.

"Let's go home," she whispered.

Epilogue

"Did you get the mail?"

"Here it is." Melanie dropped the letters on the kitchen table and walked over to kiss her husband who was washing his hands at the kitchen sink. "You smell like wood," she said, inhaling the sharp scent with pleasure. "Are you almost done with the kitchen cabinets?"

"Just have to put the panels together for the pantry doors and I can install them. Graydon will be happy when I've finished with Mom's house, I'm sure."

"So will your mom. I'm glad she agreed to let us build her a place on the yard. It's nice to have her close by."

Adam dried his hands on a towel and set it on the counter. He drew Melanie into his arms and kissed her lightly. "You look tired, Melanie Engler. How was work?"

"Busy. Thankfully I have tomorrow off. I can get

the painting done then.'' She looked past him out the window.

Helen was bent over in the garden, Tiffany hopping alongside counting the rows of beans. Melanie had to smile. ''The garden is looking even better than last year. Mom has quite a green thumb.''

''And is only too glad to give it some practice.'' Adam brushed a light kiss over Melanie's forehead, then picked up the mail.

''Well, well. Would you look at this.'' He dropped the other letters, pulled out a jacknife from the leather case on his belt and slit one envelope open, then handed it to her with a smile.

''You get to see it first.''

Melanie glanced at the return address.

The Shewchuk family.

She pulled out a letter, her fingers trembling with excitement and a touch of nervousness. A picture fell out on the table.

Melanie picked it up, and simply stared.

A family portrait.

She set it carefully on the table and started to read.

It had taken a while, the enclosed letter said, but with some counseling and time and God's grace over them all, the Shewchuks were now together again as a family.

Melanie's eyes prickled as she picked up the picture again. Dena stood to one side, her boyfriend's arm around her. She lived in Vancouver, and she and Melanie had been writing for the past couple of months. But Dena had said nothing about this.

The tears that had threatened rolled freely down her face. "They're a family again."

"Hey, sweetheart." Adam gave her a quick hug, then laid his hand on her stomach. "We're a family, too, you know."

And that made Melanie cry even harder.

And as Adam pulled her close, she sent up a prayer of thanks to God that so many hearts had turned toward home.

*   *   *   *   *

Dear Reader,

Just like the letters that Jason had written his wife, God is constantly trying to call us back to Himself. But like Adam, we wander away, thinking we don't deserve what He has to give us. But when we turn away from God, we rob ourselves. God wants us to lay our burdens on Him. We can't carry them ourselves. Our only true rest comes in Him. I pray that if you are burdened with guilt, like Adam, or if you are burdened at all, that you will allow God to take that off your shoulders. Allow His love to forgive and heal.

Carolyne Aarsen

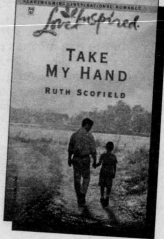

TAKE MY HAND

BY
RUTH SCOFIELD

Being a single parent was more difficult than
James Sullivan had expected, and he returned to his
long-lost faith for guidance. But was his young son's
teacher, Alexis Richmond, the answer to his prayers?
And would their newfound love be strong enough to
overcome Alexis's painful past and give her the
family she'd always dreamed of?

Don't miss
TAKE MY HAND
On sale August 2003.

Available at your favorite retail outlet.

Visit us at www.steeplehill.com

LITMH

SAMANTHA'S GIFT

BY

VALERIE HANSEN

The local teacher was showing Sean Bates around town and the gossips were working overtime, creating a romance between the new guidance counselor and teacher Rachel Woodward. But when little Samantha entered their lives, Rachel knew Sean would make a perfect father…and husband, leaving her wondering if God would have a place for Rachel in this budding family.

Don't miss

SAMANTHA'S GIFT

On sale August 2003.

Available at your favorite retail outlet.

Visit us at www.steeplehill.com   LISG

Love Inspired

A LOVE BEYOND

BY

KATE WELSH

HEARTWARMING INSPIRATIONAL ROMANCE

Love Inspired

A LOVE BEYOND

KATE WELSH

Jim Lovell was hiding something…and Crystal Alton knew it. His rugged charm couldn't hide the fact that her inquisitive new ranch hand could barely ride a horse. But would the secret he kept—that he was a detective on assignment—keep Jim from the paradise God had shown him with Crystal?

Don't miss

A LOVE BEYOND

On sale August 2003.

Available at your favorite retail outlet.

Visit us at www.steeplehill.com

LIALB